"Hello, Mystery."
Just two words

Two words in that rich smooth voice that rocked Jessica's composure.

It was as if the past nine years had been stripped away; she felt once more like a girl of eighteen standing at the college gates with Daniel Tyson's hand on her arm, restraining her when she would have pulled away.

"Here, let me take those." The deep voice was solicitous, his concern apparently genuine as he eased the wineglasses from her clenched fingers. But a gleam of amusement lurked in the depth of his eyes.

He had known all along who she was! During that confrontation in her restaurant, when she'd been totally unaware of his identity, he had known only too well that she was the Jessica Terry he'd once called some of the foulest names under the sun.

In the disturbed whirlpool of her thoughts was a tiny stream of pleasure. He *hadn't* found her completely forgettable.

Kate Walker chose the Brontë sisters, the development of their writing from childhood to maturity, as the topic for her master's thesis. It is little wonder, then, that she should go on to write romance fiction. She lives in the United Kingdom with her husband and son, and when she isn't writing, she tries to keep up with her hobbies of embroidery, knitting, antiques and, of course, reading.

Books by Kate Walker

HARLEQUIN ROMANCE

HARLEQUIN PRESENTS

JESTER'S GIRL

Kate Walker

Harlequin Books

TORONTO • NEW YORK • LONDON
AMSTERDAM • PARIS • SYDNEY • HAMBURG
STOCKHOLM • ATHENS • TOKYO • MILAN

Original hardcover edition published in 1989
by Mills & Boon Limited

ISBN 0-373-03078-9

Harlequin Romance first edition September 1990

CHAPTER ONE

IF IT had been any other sort of day, then perhaps Jessica wouldn't have made quite so much fuss about the tie. Later, she was to reflect that if she had realised who the man was she would have had second and even third thoughts about tackling him, principle or no principle. But of course she hadn't known, and it had been the sort of Monday that would have reduced even the mild-tempered Miriam to a state in which she was ready to pick a fight with the nearest available victim.

But Miriam hadn't been there, leaving the restaurant slightly short-staffed, and that had been one of the problems. From the moment Miriam had arrived at work it had been obvious that her friend and invaluable as-sistant manager was under the weather, her thin face white and strained, and in less than an hour she had admitted defeat and reluctantly accepted Jessica's offer of a taxi home. From then on the day had degenerated into total chaos, with food supplies not arriving or ap-pearing in a totally different form from the one in which they had been ordered, the heating going on the blink—a major disaster on a bitterly cold January day—and Bill, the chef, and normally the most placid of men, throwing an uncharacteristic tantrum and declaring that he couldn't possibly work in the noise and disorder of the necessary repairs.

To cap it all, Jessica herself was not in the best frame of mind to handle any sort of crisis, her feelings still raw and smarting after the way Jack had broken off their relationship the previous night.

'But *why*?' Miriam had exclaimed when Jessica had told her what had happened. 'You seemed like the perfect couple to me.'

Jessica had thought so too, and that was why the break-up had hit her so hard. She wasn't in love with Jack, or he with her, but they had jelled together from the start. Both in their late twenties—Jack, at twenty-eight, just a year older than Jessica herself—both active, busy, successful people, they worked hard at their jobs and enjoyed an equally full social life, one she had enjoyed and had hoped to continue, so Jack's abrupt announcement had stunned her.

'What happened?'

Miriam's expression was disturbed. Still deeply in love with her husband after six years of marriage, she was a true romantic at heart, wanting everyone to find the happiness she had with Al—though just lately her own marriage seemed to have been going through a rough patch, something Miriam was reluctant to discuss in any detail.

'What exactly did Jack say?'

'That it had been good, but now it was over.' Jessica echoed his words drily.

'That's all?'

That was all Jack had said, but personally Jessica had a few other ideas on the matter. She strongly suspected that sex had a major part to play in the break-up of the relationship. Jack was the sort of man who took his pleasures as seriously as he did his business deals, and she believed that he had taken her refusal to sleep with him rather less well than he would ever admit. It wasn't Jack Ryan's style to play the heavy macho male. He made a great thing about being liberated and appreciating a woman's right to say no—particularly in today's sexual climate—but, deep down, her persistent refusal had irked and frustrated him.

'I can see his point,' Jessica said slowly. 'It was fun while it lasted, but it wasn't going anywhere.'

If it *had* been going anywhere, would she have been more willing to accede to Jack's attempts to get her into bed? After all, she had sexual feelings, like any other woman, and Jack couldn't be said to leave her cold. He was a particularly good-looking man.

Jessica gave herself a mental shake. Jack hadn't left her cold, but he certainly hadn't raised her temperature wildly, either. It had been all too easy to resist his attempts at seduction, and that was why the relationship had been going nowhere.

But all the same, it had come as a shock to find that someone she regarded as being part of her life and whose company she had enjoyed no longer wanted to be with her, and those feelings had been aggravated by the normal January blues, the inevitable post New Year letdown that had set in with the short, dark days and long, cold nights. That feeling was hard to cope with, and so when John Bennett, an old friend whom, like Miriam, she had known from her schooldays, phoned during the afternoon, his tone of voice revealing that he was feeling as low as Jessica herself, she had impulsively invited him to have dinner with her that evening. John had just been through a very painful divorce and was clearly in need of some company.

But, before the meal was even half-way through, Jessica began to regret her charitable impulse, because it soon became evident that John had read more into her invitation than she had ever intended. From the moment she had told him that she and Jack had split up, he hung on her every word, his brown eyes fixed on her face with an expression strongly reminiscent of a spaniel puppy her mother had once owned, in a way that made her wonder uneasily if perhaps he had some hope of replacing Jack in her life.

She sincerely hoped not. Any attraction he might feel towards her would be simply on the rebound from his broken marriage, and right now that was a complication she could well do without. But how could she get that fact across without further bruising to his already fragile ego?

The sudden opening of the restaurant door provided a welcome diversion, drawing Jessica's eyes as a tall, masculine figure strode into the restaurant and approached the reception desk. She had time to acknowledge the immediate and forceful appeal of a pair of straight, broad shoulders under a battered leather jacket, and a gleaming mane of dark hair, tousled by the savage wind outside, before, clearly determined to draw her attention back to him, John leaned forward and took her hand in his.

'You're looking spectacularly beautiful tonight, Jess. That dress really suits you.'

'That's very sweet of you, John. Thank you.'

As she inclined her head in acknowledgement of the compliment, Jessica smoothly extricated her fingers from under John's to make a minor and unnecessary adjustment to the sleeve of her red linen dress. Its bright colour was a departure from the norm for her; usually she stuck to pastels, but she had seen the dress in her favourite boutique just before Christmas and, probably influenced by the bright reds and greens of the festive season, had decided on impulse to try it on.

She had been amazed to see the effect it had had on her pale, creamy skin, throwing colour on to her high cheekbones so that her wide, grey eyes looked huge and softly glowing above them. Her hair had been longer then. At New Year she had had several inches lopped of the golden-blonde mane so that it now hung in a sleek, glowing bell around her oval-shaped face.

Remembering how, only a few months before, John had described his wife, a petite redhead, as the most beautiful woman in the world, Jessica privately took the liberty of doubting that her own tall, curvaceous figure would hold any real appeal for him. 'Statuesque' was the term she would have used to describe herself if asked, though Jack's favourite word had been 'voluptuous'. A touch of cynicism at the thought of the probable motives of both men made her mouth twist slightly, and as she turned her head to hide her expression from John she was thoroughly disconcerted to find herself looking straight into the eyes of the man at the reception desk, their coolly assessing expression unnerving, making her heart jolt uncomfortably in shock.

Where was Tracey? she wondered with more than a touch of irritation, thankfully breaking that disturbing contact as she looked around for the receptionist. Luckily, at that moment Tracey appeared from Jessica's office, and she was able to turn her attention back to John.

'Are there any good plays on at the Civic?' she asked, rushing into conversation with a haste that betrayed, if only to herself, how ridiculously upsetting she had found that probing, appraising gaze. She should be flattered, really, to think that she had drawn the stranger's eyes, that he found her attractive. But somehow simple attraction wasn't the effect that that clear, direct gaze had communicated. It had been a hard-eyed stare, and strangely critical, with something worryingly close to contempt in it, an emotion for which she could find no possible explanation. 'I thought I might treat myself to a really good seat if there's something worth watching now that the pantomime season's over. Jack was never very keen——'

Too late, she realised that her words could be interpreted as encouragement, a hint that she would not be averse to the offer of a date, and, sure enough, John took her up on them enthusiastically.

'I'd be glad to take you any time. As a matter of fact, I was thinking of going this week. One of the lads in the office was saying that there's a comedian who's well worth seeing. He didn't mention his name, but——'

'A comedian?' Jessica broke in with unnecessary emphasis, her only concern being to correct any misunderstanding her earlier words had caused. 'I don't think that's my sort of thing at all. Do you mean a stand-up comic—a working-men's club sort of act?'

'Not exactly.'

John looked taken aback at her vehemence—as well he might, Jessica thought wryly, hardly recognising her own voice in the sharp, crisp tones that carried clearly across the quiet room, cutting into the murmur of conversation from the few occupied tables.

'He has played a few clubs, but now he's touring the theatres. He's got quite a reputation——'

'I'll bet he has.'

She'd started on this now, she was going to have to carry it through. She didn't want to be caught in the trap of John's hurt feelings, but it was probably kinder to let him think it was the show she objected to, not him personally. When the suspicion that there was more to it than that, that the brief, disturbing contact with the new arrival had unsettled her more than she cared to admit slid into her mind, she pushed it away hastily.

'I can just imagine the sort of thing—some fat slob of a man, probably three parts drunk, telling tasteless blue jokes and making racist comments——'

'Not really——' John tried to protest.

But Jessica wasn't listening. Hunting for a way of avoiding the conversation, avoiding the way it was heading, she had glanced up again to where the man who had come into the restaurant was standing, his appearance providing her with welcome inspiration.

'Just a minute, John.'

In one swift, decisive movement she was out of her chair and moving purposefully across the room.

'Excuse me——'

He was involved in some conversation with Tracey, and took the time—rather pointedly, Jessica felt—to finish what he was saying before, turning slowly, he directed an enquiring glance at her. Those few moments gave Jessica just long enough to pause and consider exactly what had fired her newly determined mood.

She had wanted to end the difficult conversation with John, true, and the point she wanted to raise was one she held strongly, but there was more to it than that. In the moment she had turned and met that coolly contemptuous gaze, the hairs on the back of her neck had lifted like those of a wary cat faced with a hostile intruder into its private territory, and the unsettled, antagonistic mood that had gripped her made her want to score a point against this insolent creature in a way that defied logic or any form of rational thought.

'Yes?'

Seen up close, Jessica realised, his hair wasn't as dark as she had at first believed it to be, but was shot through with glints of glowing chestnut, thick and wavy in a slightly unruly way. In her high heels she was almost exactly the same height as him, and the eyes that looked straight into hers were light, the colour that was usually described as hazel, but which could be brown or green depending on the light. Right now, they were amber-coloured, the heavy lids drooping slightly at the outer corners in a way that gave him a sleepily sensual look that was singularly attractive.

'Can I help you?'

It was a devastating voice, the sort of rich baritone that, totally irrationally, made Jessica want to reply, Yes, I hope so—I really hope so. With a mental shake she made herself concentrate on her original reason for approaching him.

'I don't know if you realise it, but there's a house rule here——'

For some inexplicable reason her voice faltered as she looked into those changeable eyes that were now fixed on her face with a disconcerting directness. There was no overt hostility in that mildly enquiring gaze, and yet she felt something shivering over her nerves like the intuitive response of some small animal sensing the presence of a hunting predator. That lazily tolerant expression seemed to hide the power and strength of an indolent tiger, one that was making up its mind whether it was worth the effort of pouncing or not, and the stranger's muscled frame, tousled dark hair and the well-worn leather jacket suddenly seemed alien and somehow threatening in the cool elegance of the restaurant's green and white décor.

'A house rule,' he prompted softly, his blatantly falsely patient smile sending a prickle of irritation running over her skin.

'Yes.' The single syllable came out clipped and curt, uncharacteristically cold as ice. 'Gentlemen are not admitted to the restaurant without a tie.'

Jessica directed a pointed glance at the neckline of his cream cotton shirt, left casually open at the throat, revealing a powerful neck and the beginning of a firmly muscled chest.

The man's eyes followed her gaze and his wide, mobile mouth twitched slightly at the corners as if he was trying to suppress either anger or amusement—but which one Jessica couldn't begin to guess. Either was possible, but neither seemed particularly understandable in the circumstances.

'How very old-fashioned.'

The satirically drawled comment took her aback for a moment. It wasn't at all what she had expected. Most people in Scarby, and certainly all of her regulars, knew of the rule that ties were to be worn and followed it strictly. On the few occasions she had had to enforce it, her approach had usually been met with an apologetic admission that the man concerned simply hadn't known that the rule existed, followed by an immediate departure, but neither an apology nor a swift exit seemed to be in this man's mind at all.

'It's not old-fashioned at all. It's simply that we prefer a certain standard of dress here.'

When she had opened the Jester, Jessica had been determined that the restaurant would be a place where people could enjoy their evening out, with all the elegance and dressing-up that that entailed. She deplored the casual attitudes that currently prevailed, the custom of wearing anything—usually the ubiquitous denim jeans—anywhere, feeling that it took all the romance and style out of an event, and she had resolved that her restaurant at least would not succumb to that particular trend.

'If you want a quick snack, there's a pizza parlour just down the road.'

That sardonic, 'How very old-fashioned,' still stung, making her voice tart, and from the way his mouth twisted she knew that her tone had not been lost on him.

'I don't like Italian food—and no, I wasn't just looking for a "quick snack".' Once more dry satire laced his voice as he quoted her own words back at her, and Jessica had the unnerving feeling that he was deliberately trying to provoke her. 'I've been travelling all day, I want a decent meal, and I was told that this was the best restaurant in town.'

Jessica would not have been human if she hadn't felt a swift rush of delight at his words, but she clamped down hard on the inclination to smile her pleasure straight into those amber eyes. Did he think that the offhand compliment would win her round, flatter her into forgetting the house rule just this once?

Very likely he did, she reflected cynically, and quite possibly he also believed that his own undeniable good looks would win round any female with whom he came into conflict. She'd met men of his type all too often, men who believed that a flashing smile, a cajoling note in the voice, would sway any weak feminine heart. The voice he had, there was no doubt about that, but she had to admit that, surprisingly, no smile had yet been in evidence, and that made her think of the moment she had looked up, her eyes meeting his, the unsettled, uneasy feeling reawakening as she recalled the look of contempt she had seen on his face.

'Then you'll appreciate that we have certain standards that we want to maintain.'

Those changeable eyes flickered over her tautly controlled face in a way that sent a sensation like the prickle of pins and needles running down her spine, before they swung away again in the direction of John Bennett, who was sitting back in his chair, watching the scene before him with a rather bemused expression on his thin face.

'I'm sure you don't need me to point out that the gentleman you were sitting with isn't dressed according to these so-important standards.'

With a sense of shock Jessica realised that it was true. She had been so pleased to see John, to see anyone who might bring her out of the restless and despondent mood that had plagued her all day, that she hadn't registered the fact that, although his shirt was closely buttoned up to the neck, he wore no tie. And the suspicion that he might be angling for a date had so occupied her mind that she hadn't noticed that lack—until now.

'Mr Bennett is here as my guest.'

Her inner irritation at the way she had been subtly edged into a corner combined with fury at her own mistake to make her voice cold and haughty in a way that clearly disconcerted Tracey, who was listening shamelessly to the whole conversation.

Keen, penetrating hazel eyes swung back to her face. 'And you are——?'

Jessica drew herself up, meeting that insolent gaze with a degree of equanimity that she hoped concealed the disjointed state of her thoughts. She was beginning to feel distinctly rattled, and that worried her. Normally she could handle any situation that arose—after all, she'd been her own boss for nearly four years now. But there was something about this man that set her nerves on edge.

Even more disturbing was the way that her mood was beginning to feel strangely familiar. Did she know this man? Or was there something about him that reminded her of someone she had once known and disliked intensely?

'My name is Jessica Terry. I'm the owner and manageress of this restaurant.'

There was more than a touch of pride in her voice. Established on a shoestring budget, the Jester had taken every penny she possessed and had absorbed almost every waking second of her day at the beginning, but now it was one of the most popular eating-places in Scarby. The name had been derived from the first two syllables of her own name, and from the first it had seemed as if the medieval Fool, with his parti-coloured doublet and hose, cap and bells, whose figure adorned the brightly painted sign above the restaurant's door, had become her personal good luck charm. Certainly, she had never looked back from the moment she had adopted it, and among her friends and regular customers she was known affectionately as 'the Jester's Girl'.

He showed no sign of surprise at her announcement, she'd give him that. Even in these liberated days, most people asked to speak to the *manager*, expecting to see a man. But the small point Jessica had chalked up in the stranger's favour was immediately erased by the anger that washed over her as she saw those clear eyes slide down over her body in a lazily appreciative survey, lingering blatantly on the curves of her figure under the red linen dress.

She was well used to men weighing her up in this way; it was one of the problems of being a career woman. There were few of the male sex who would accept her simply in her business capacity, without judging her from the sexual point of view too, and she had developed a cool, dismissive gaze to handle such situations. She used it now on the man before her, her wide grey eyes meeting his with total control, in spite of the fact that a mini volcano of anger was bubbling inside her, threatening to throw her off balance completely.

Why did this particular man disturb her so much? She'd coped with his type before, coped easily and successfully, and gone on her way without turning a hair—so why should he rile her in this way?

'Well, then, as *manageress*——' he emphasised the word in an ironical echo of her own tone 'has it ever occurred to you that if you put rather more emphasis on welcoming customers to this place, instead of imposing petty and archaic rules about the way they dress, you might attract a larger clientele?'

The sarcastic question was accompanied by a swift, expressive flick of a glance around the room, taking in the number of empty tables, the waitresses standing idle, before swinging back to her, his look of deceptively mild enquiry clearly designed to provoke—and succeeding only too well, Jessica admitted privately as her hand itched to wipe it from his face. She was sure now that he was playing with her and that, like a cat with a mouse, he fully intended to drag out the moments of his perverse pleasure to the full.

It was true that the restaurant wasn't exactly crowded, there was no way she could deny that, but that was only the post-holiday slump. Everyone had spent too much over Christmas and the New Year, and after the whirl of office parties and firms' dinners, many of which the Jester had catered for, most of her regular customers were content simply to stay at home and keep warm.

How I run my business is no concern of yours, she was tempted to retort but, mindful of the few customers she did have, some of whom were already beginning to take an interest in the unusually prolonged conversation, she swallowed the words down with an effort and managed a coolly insincere smile.

'The Jester is clearly not the sort of place you thought it was,' she said, her voice dripping honeyed sarcasm. 'So, if you'd just——' She made a gesture towards the door.

'Hold on a minute,' he cut in on her swiftly, something suspiciously close to laughter lurking in his eyes, making them gleam like the stone in a ring she had at home.

Tiger's eye, she remembered it was called, the name making her recall her earlier, fanciful connection of him with a jungle cat, and sending a tiny frisson of apprehension feathering across her nerves. She should have known that he wasn't going to let her win as easily as that. Had the tiger decided to spring, after all?

'If I want to eat here, I need a tie—right?'

Jessica managed a stiff nod. She had the unnerving feeling of having bitten off rather more than she could chew, and that didn't make for an easy reply.

'OK——'

He turned to Tracey, whose eyes were wide and bright with an intrigued delight that she tried hastily and unsuccessfully to hide.

'I really am most devastatingly hungry——'

The bronze-coloured eyes locked with Tracey's blue ones, skilfully projecting the impression that, at that moment, she was the most important person in the room for him in a way that clearly entranced the younger girl, while it made Jessica feel sick at his blatant and deliberate manipulation.

'And I would very much like to eat before I collapse completely from a total lack of nourishment—I've driven a long way to get here today. But it appears that I am— *improperly dressed*——' he laced the words with silky satire '—for this exclusive establishment, so——'

His eyes flicked to Jessica briefly, then back again and, alerted by the tiny movement, she looked at Tracey more closely, seeing at once exactly what he was after. The younger girl was smartly dressed in a neat black skirt and black silk blouse—and around her neck she wore a decorative tie made up of hundreds of tiny imitation pearls stitched together.

'So I wondered——' that beautiful voice deepened, became enticingly, seductively husky '—if you would let me borrow your tie, just for an hour or so?'

How could anyone resist that appeal? Even as she seethed with impotent fury, Jessica had to admit to the pull of an instinctive attraction that tugged at her heart— and Tracey certainly couldn't withstand the gentle cajolery, it was clear. Her hands were already going to the clasp at the back of her neck, when an abrupt movement that Jessica was unable to control reminded her of her employer's presence, and she turned an uncertain glance in the older girl's direction.

'Or would that mean that this young lady would then not be suitably dressed, too? I'd hate to get her into any trouble.'

The act was almost convincing. His expression was one of genuine concern, but his eyes betrayed him, the gleam of amused triumph glowing in them like a flame.

Jessica had to grit her teeth against the angry retort that, No, Tracey would most definitely not be suitably dressed.

'Miss Anderson is always very properly dressed,' she bit out, knowing there was nothing else she could say.

Her face wreathed in smiles, Tracey finished unfastening the tie and handed it over, a rosy pink shading her cheeks as the man returned his attention to her, switching on the smile Jessica had earlier expected him to use.

That smile would have entranced any woman. Jessica herself found it infuriatingly difficult to control a response that came disturbingly close to jealousy as she saw the sparkle in the other girl's eyes, the way her colour deepened to a fiery blush. The shock of that unexpected emotion kept Jessica silent as, without a trace of self-consciousness, the man buttoned up his shirt and fastened the delicate tie around his neck.

There was nothing she *could* say, Jessica repeated to herself. The rule said a tie—it didn't specify what *sort* of tie—and, besides, she had had quite enough of this confrontation—and of this man. All she wanted was to have the whole incident over and done with—and she still had John and his unwanted invitation to deal with.

Determinedly schooling her expression into one of carefully controlled indifference, she refused to let herself look at the man again, only too aware of the mocking triumph she would see in those clear eyes if she did. The only way out of this with any kind of dignity was to pretend that it had never happened.

'Would you show the gentleman to a table, please, Tracey?' she managed coolly enough, though that 'gentleman' stuck in her throat. She was glad that none of her internal disturbance showed in her voice, which was as calm and controlled as she could have wished.

Courtesy forced her to add, 'Enjoy your meal,' before she turned back to her own table, her head held erect, her spine stiff because, although she couldn't see him, she knew that the man was watching her, she could almost feel the force of his gaze on her, burning into her back through the material of her dress as she rejoined John. She was only thankful to have escaped with her self-control and her pride intact.

CHAPTER TWO

FROM then on it was impossible to finish what was left of her meal, though Jessica knew that Bill would be mortally insulted by the amount of food she had left on her plate, and her concentration on what John was saying was practically nil. She couldn't understand her feelings, couldn't believe that one small confrontation of the sort she handled every day could have destroyed her equanimity so completely.

No, it wasn't just this particular episode; it was the way she had been feeling all day. It had started with the mood of restlessness and dissatisfaction that had been the result of Jack's abrupt departure from her life—and Miriam being out of sorts hadn't helped.

Jessica frowned her concern as she recalled her friend's reluctance to go home.

'It's just the time of the month, Jess,' she had protested. 'I'd much rather be here than at home. Al's working overtime again and the house seems so empty without him.'

Miriam's husband always seemed to be working these days, Jessica reflected. Probably the cause of their problems was his excessive devotion to his work, which meant that his wife hardly ever saw him. And poor Miriam's problems today were probably compounded by disappointment. Jessica knew that she and Al wanted a large family but, going by today's events, this month at least they had been unsuccessful.

22

Then, of course, there had been the problem of John and his unwanted attentions. The insolent stranger's arrival had just been the last straw, one final difficulty at the end of an already fraught day.

Jessica's eyes slid to where the dark-haired man sat in the corner of the room, still wearing that ridiculous tie with the sort of panache that made it impossible to find his appearance even remotely funny. It was a pity he was such an oaf. With looks like his he could easily be a real charmer; those strongly carved features would be a gift to the latest television mini-series.

What *did* he do? His appearance gave little clue to his possible occupation. He had said that he'd driven a long way to get to Scarby, so was he some sort of sales rep? On consideration, Jessica decided that that was not the answer. He looked nothing like any rep she had ever seen. That leather jacket was battered with age, and the cream shirt and dark brown trousers he wore with it were totally anonymous, the sort of thing that could be worn by anyone in their off-duty hours. But he was eating at the Jester, which presupposed an adequate income at least.

'You didn't recognise him, did you?' John's low-toned voice intruded on her thoughts.

'Who?' she asked, forcing her attention back to him, thoroughly disconcerted by the way her mind had latched on to the stranger like a terrier on a rat, and seemed to have no intention of letting go, in spite of her determined efforts to the contrary.

'Tyson.' Seeing her blank look, John elucidated further. 'Daniel Tyson.'

'Daniel Tyson?' Jessica echoed faintly, her mind working overtime, searching through her memories until at last she came up with the recollection of her college

days, when she was just eighteen. Immediately she wished
she hadn't remembered.

'Daniel Tyson!' she repeated on a very different note.

'The very same,' John confirmed. 'Don't tell me you'd
forgotten him.'

But she *had* forgotten—or perhaps her mind had
blown a fuse, wanting to erase the past, refusing to
remember. Now that name rang all sorts of bells in her
mind, loud and discordant like a warning peal, as she
recalled how the stranger had seemed naggingly familiar.
Deep inside her, some tiny part of her mind had remembered that voice, those mocking hazel eyes.

'Don't you remember when he used to live here?'

Oh, yes, now she remembered—and devoutly wished
she hadn't. She had just started her catering course at
the local college, and half-way through the autumn term
a new student had joined the A-level group, a boy a year
or two older than most of his classmates who, the college
grapevine said, had originally left school at seventeen,
without taking his exams, and had now decided to re-
sit them. Other than that, no one knew anything about
him—why he'd come there, where he'd come from.

It was no wonder that, earlier, Jessica had mentally
connected the insolent 'stranger' with television. Sub-
consciously even then her mind must have begun to
recognise him, because that was what his father had
done. Melvyn Tyson had been a star in one of television's most popular soap operas, and he had bought a
huge mansion in one of the nearby villages.

Jessica remembered how the whole college had buzzed
with excitement when that particular fact had come to
light, the news spreading like wildfire. She herself had
experienced a painful kickback from that particular dis-

covery, one that made her squirm inside at the thought of it.

At eighteen, tall, blonde and with a figure that even then had been well-developed, making other girls in her class look almost boyish by comparison, Jessica had revelled in the attention her looks brought her. The only daughter in a family of four children, she had grown up accustomed to male interest and approval, and as a result, embarrassing though it was to admit it, had become an inveterate and indiscriminate flirt, dating whoever took her fancy, supremely confident that every male in the college would want to be seen with her. And she had been right, they all fell under her spell—all of them except for Daniel Tyson.

He had joined the college just before half-term, and had very soon earned himself a reputation as something of a mystery man, a loner who worked hard and avoided most of the students' social events in a way that made it even more curious that he had left school so early, when he was obviously a model student.

Inevitably, this image of mystery and unapproach-ability had meant that Daniel Tyson had come to be re-garded as something of a challenge, the boy whose attention every girl wanted, all of them hoping that 1they would be the one to break down the invisible barriers with which he seemed to surround himself. Among Jessica's friends it was assumed that it was only a matter of time before she and Daniel became a couple, and her pride had taken a severe knock when, in spite of her offering every encouragement in the form of smiling, teasing comments or openly flirtatious glances, he had blatantly ignored her.

The discovery that Melvyn Tyson was Daniel's father had only added to the feminine rivalry, and Jessica had been subjected to some sharply satirical comments from Erica Stanton, her main rival for the title of most popular girl in the college.

'Think you're God's gift to men, don't you, Terry?' Erica had sneered. 'You think you can get any man you like—but Melvyn Tyson's son just isn't interested.'

Her pride stung, Jessica wasn't prepared to take that lying down, and with the Christmas disco looming on the horizon she had rushed headlong into unthinking action. What had followed had been one of the most painfully humiliating episodes of her whole life. It was no wonder her subconscious had tried to bury it as deeply as possible.

'*That* Daniel Tyson,' she said, resisting the temptation to turn her head and look at the man on the opposite side of the room.

Had Tyson recognised her, or had he, like her, buried their previous meetings in the mists of time? The trouble was that she didn't know how she felt about that. One part of her wanted the memory of those long-ago days to be blotted out, lost forever, but another, less rational side to her mind was piqued to think that she could be so easily forgotten.

'I suppose he's come back to visit his father,' she said, because she had to say *something*, even though her mind was preoccupied with the private Pandora's box of memories that that name had opened up.

'I doubt it.' John's carefully low voice was cynical, his mouth twisting in evident distaste. 'Whatever they may say about prodigal sons, I doubt that Melvyn Tyson would be willing to welcome that particular black sheep back into the fold. Don't you remember how he disappeared from Scarby?'

'Disappeared? John, he went to university.'

'That was the official story. I happen to know the truth.'

John glanced swiftly across the room to where the subject of their conversation sat, oblivious to the fact that he was being discussed, and his voice sank to a whisper.

'Before he died, my father was Melvyn Tyson's friend. They used to play golf together, and they'd often have a drink in the club-house afterwards. One day Tyson got rather drunk. He'd been knocking back whisky, and was clearly upset about something, so naturally Dad asked what the problem was. Tyson told him that he'd thrown his son out of his house. He'd been on a trip to London, and came home unexpectedly early to find Daniel in bed with his stepmother—his father's wife.'

Jessica felt sick, a sour taste filling her mouth. For her own personal reasons she disliked Daniel Tyson intensely, but *this* was something else entirely. What sort of man could behave in that way? She tried to imagine how her father might feel if one of her brothers had done something similar, and the queasy sensation grew worse. When she thought of the way Tyson had treated her——

And now that louse was sitting here, in her restaurant, totally at ease... Her eyes, bright with suppressed anger, flew to the man she now knew as Daniel Tyson, and she struggled with the impulse to get to her feet, march over to him and demand that he leave at once, tell him to his face that she didn't want his type in here. How dared he? How dared he just walk in and——?

Her thought processes froze as, at that moment, as if feeling her gaze on him, Daniel Tyson looked up, meeting her eyes with a composure that was not mirrored on Jessica's face as her mind hazed in embarrassment at being caught watching him like that. Fury replaced discomfort as, clearly taking her angry stare for one of sensual interest, he reached for his wineglass and lifted it in a mocking toast. With a sharp exclamation of anger and disgust, Jessica hurriedly looked away again, directing her attention towards John with a determination and concentration that clearly disconcerted—and delighted—him.

'What about this theatre trip, then?' he asked, taking her sudden interest as an indication that his invitation was more welcome than he had at first believed. 'Would you like to come?'

Jessica almost groaned aloud. Why did he have to be so persistent? It seemed ironic that only that morning she had been upset because of the lack of masculine company in her life. Now, all she could think was that she wanted these two particular males to leave—as soon as possible.

'To see this comedian? No, thanks, John.'

The time for tact was over, she decided. She had to get her message across clearly and unambiguously. It didn't matter that she had never seen this comic in her life. She was prepared to say anything, just as long as John got the point.

'I can't think of anything I'd like less,' she said crisply. 'I've no desire to spend an evening watching some crude, arrogant, tasteless bore who just happens to think he's funny.'

It was with a strong sense of relief that she saw John leave, but that relief was mixed with guilt. She liked John, as a friend, but nothing more. In her present unsettled mood she couldn't cope with being a shoulder for him to cry on, someone he could turn to on the rebound from his wife's rejection. But she could have handled things better—and probably would have done so if the memories that Daniel Tyson's name evoked hadn't rattled her so badly.

Silently she cursed the man in the corner, once more struggling with the impulse to demand that he leave. She strongly suspected that he had watched John's discomfited departure and, remembering the accusations he had flung at her in the past, she was unable to stop herself from wondering just what interpretation he had put on it—if he remembered the past, of course. He had shown no sign of recognition towards her. Hot anger threatened to boil up inside her and spill out like lava from a volcano at the thought of what John had told her. Daniel Tyson had called her some of the foulest names under the sun, but all the time his own conscience had been far from clear. If she had known then what she knew now——

It took every ounce of her determination to force herself to concentrate once more on her work, resolving to put Daniel Tyson out of her mind once and for all; but all the determination in the world couldn't stop her from noticing when he finally pushed back his chair and strolled over to the cash desk to pay his bill. It didn't stop her being aware of the fact that the simple transaction was taking an inordinately long time, and her mood was aggravated by a sudden sharp stab deep inside at the thought that he was probably chatting up Tracey, possibly even offering her a date as a way of thanking her for the loan of the tie, which he had just handed back to her with another of those devastatingly seductive smiles.

Calm down, Jessica told herself fiercely. She had only to wait a few more minutes and he would be gone—out of her life for good, she hoped. He was hardly likely to

be staying in Scarby, knowing how his father must feel
about him. Just a few more minutes, she repeated as
Daniel Tyson straightened up.

But instead of turning towards the door as she had
expected—and hoped—she saw to her horror that he was
heading straight for her. Immediately, with a brusque,
awkward movement that betrayed her feelings too
closely, she hurried to his table and began piling plates
together with the sort of noisy clatter that would have
driven her to make a stern reproof if any of the waitresses
had been responsible for it.

'Miss Terry——'

She couldn't speak to him, she felt her throat would
close up if she even tried. But to ignore him would be
an admission of the way he had affected her, which was
something she would hate him to realise.

'Yes?'

The enquiring glance she turned in his direction was
so brief as to be positively insulting, and she kept her
hands busy all the time, stacking the dirty china and
cutlery on a tray. He had left a very generous tip, she
noticed automatically, unreasoningly furious at the
thought that she could find no fault with him over that.

'I just wanted you—as the manageress of this restaurant—to know that I enjoyed my meal very much.'

Belatedly, Jessica's instinctive courtesy surfaced,
soothing some of her ruffled feelings.

'Thank you. I'll tell Bill, our chef, that. He takes our
customers' comments very much to heart.'

The compliment was the last thing she had expected,
her body having tensed in anticipation of some further
satirical comment. It was only as she allowed herself to
relax that she registered the subtle emphasis on the word
'meal'.

'And I found your staff extremely helpful.'

Your *staff*. Once more his intonation said more than his actual words, stinging sharply at the realisation of his deliberate exclusion of herself. Was he needling her in this way simply because of the confrontation they had had over what he considered a petty and archaic rule of dress, or *did* he remember her? And, if so, was he trying to provoke her into remembering, too?

Daniel Tyson had always had an acid tongue, as she knew to her cost, having been on the receiving end of it. But this subtle taunting was something new. Nine years ago, there had been nothing subtle about his approach—it had been a full-scale broadside attack.

If he *was* trying to provoke her into remembering him, then she was going to make him think he had failed, she resolved. That would be the best possible sort of revenge. Recalling her own sense of pique at being thought so very unmemorable, she could imagine what the same feeling would do to a man of Daniel Tyson's ego. Once more she switched on her automatic, polite smile, suspecting that Daniel Tyson would be well aware of its insincerity.

'We aim to please,' she murmured graciously, seeing a muscle at the corner of his mouth twitch, as if her cool indifference had hit home. 'I hope you have a safe journey,' she added, in a none-too-subtle hint that his immediate departure would be very welcome. But Daniel Tyson had no hesitation in pulling that particular rug from under her feet.

'Oh, I'm not going anywhere tonight,' he told her, the smoothness of his tone only very slightly ruffled by a touch of something that, infuriatingly, Jessica suspected was a mocking laughter. 'As a matter of fact, I'm staying in Scarby for at least a week. Perhaps I'll see you again some time.'

Not if I see you first, Jessica flung after him mentally as he strolled towards the door. He couldn't be staying! His father wouldn't want him here, and she wasn't sure she could cope with the prospect of a chance meeting in the street or perhaps in the restaurant once again. If he hadn't remembered her already, how long would it be before, with once-familiar surroundings reminding him of those long-ago days, he recalled where he had heard the name Jessica Terry before? And what would his reaction be then?

As the door swung to behind him, Jessica felt her shoulders sag, and a wave of tiredness swept over her, making her feel like a puppet whose strings had been cut. Suddenly she desperately wanted to go home, thinking longingly of a hot bath and of burying the tensions of the day in the oblivion of sleep.

But there was still the restaurant to put to rights, the cashing-up to be done, and a hundred and one other jobs that would leave everything ready for morning. It was almost an hour before she spoke to Tracey again, as she collected the evening's takings ready to put in the safe.

'Another quiet night,' the younger girl commented with a wry glance at the bundle of notes on the counter. 'Mrs Higgins' Monday night out with her sister and Joan Lassiter's birthday treat hardly make for a heavy night's takings. Still, at least there was one new face——'

And what a face, her expression said. Jessica supposed it had had to come. Tracey's flushed face and glowing eyes when Daniel Tyson had spoken to her had revealed only too clearly the effect he'd had on her. It seemed impossible to believe that Jessica herself had once felt like that about him. Perhaps she should warn Tracey, tell her just what sort of a man Tyson was, but an innate reluctance to spread scandal—even about a man of his type—held her back.

'I'll finish here, Tracey, if you want to get off.'

'Oh, thanks, Miss Terry. Dad will be waiting for me— I heard his car pull up outside a few minutes ago.'

She had turned, heading for the staffroom to collect her coat, when some thought struck her and she swung back.

'I almost forgot. He left this for you.'

'For me?'

Jessica stared in some confusion at the envelope Tracey held out to her. She didn't have to ask who 'he' was; there had been only one person in the restaurant who could put that note Tracey's voice.

'Yes. He said——'

She broke off suddenly, colour rising to her cheeks, her eyes not meeting Jessica's.

'He told me to give it to the manageress,' she said hastily, obviously holding something back.

Jessica sighed. Wasn't she free of that wretched creature even now?

'I think you'd better tell me exactly what he said,' she said resignedly, knowing intuitively that whatever Daniel Tyson had said was unlikely to be pleasant.

'Oh, well...' Tracey's colour deepened. 'He said I was to say—to say it was from the "crude, arrogant, tasteless bore"——'

'What?'

Jessica's grey eyes widened in shock as she recognised her own words, spoken to John earlier in the evening, and quoted exactly.

'Thank you, Tracey.'

It was an effort to keep her voice calmly indifferent as knots of apprehension twisted her stomach, and she had to work hard not to let her hand shake, betraying her inner feelings as she took the envelope, holding it tentatively, as if she was afraid it might blow up in her face.

What had he found to write to her about? she wondered as Tracey left. Nothing complimentary, certainly. Perhaps the note was another of his tormenting little games. Had he chosen this way to reveal his identity to her, believing she hadn't recognised him, perhaps with some cynically cutting reminder of their past meetings? Jessica toyed with the idea of tearing the envelope to shreds and flinging it into the wastepaper basket, but curiosity held her back.

From the 'crude, arrogant, tasteless bore'... Had her voice carried so clearly, then? In her determination to get her message across to John, she hadn't paused to consider that her emphatic tones might be heard by anyone else. But why should Daniel Tyson think her comment had applied to him?

'Goodnight, Miss Terry.'

The two waitresses came past, buttoning up their coats and making rueful faces as they stepped out into the cold, dark night. The icy current of air that sneaked into the restaurant made Jessica start, realising how deeply her abstracted mood had gripped her.

'Oh, this is ridiculous!' she reproved herself out loud. Why was she standing here like this, afraid to open an envelope? What possible harm could a letter do, for heaven's sake?

With a determined movement she ripped open the envelope and pulled out the two beige-coloured slips of paper it contained, automatically registering the heading—'The Civic Theatre'.

Theatre tickets? *Complimentary* theatre tickets. But why?

For a long moment Jessica's numbed brain couldn't make any logical connection between the man in the restaurant and the tickets she held in her hand. Then she shook her head dazedly, focused more clearly, and a name leapt out at her with a force like a blow to her face.

Daniel Tyson—and some dates—tonight and all the rest of the week. In her mind she could hear John saying, 'I was thinking of going this week...there's a comedian who's well worth seeing.'

It couldn't be! Daniel Tyson had left Scarby for university. He couldn't be the comedian John had mentioned.

But Daniel Tyson *was* in town. His name was on the tickets—and how would he have come by *complimentary* tickets if he wasn't connected with this particular show?

It was then that the significance of her own words, used by Daniel and quoted again by Tracey, hit home, leaving her no choice but to accept that, impossible as it seemed, the comedian she had dismissed so scathingly and so audibly was the Daniel Tyson she had known and detested all those years ago. Remembering the sort of man he had been then, Jessica thought of his possible reaction to her careless words and groaned out loud in despair.

CHAPTER THREE

SHE wasn't going to use those tickets. There was no doubt in Jessica's mind about that, even though she had to admit to an undeniable streak of curiosity as to just what sort of a show Daniel Tyson's might be. Nothing would get her to that theatre, under any circumstances. But that determination was severely undermined by Miriam's reaction the next morning, when Jessica casually mentioned the tickets, carefully avoiding revealing exactly how she had come by them.

'Daniel Tyson! Oh, Jess, I'd love to see him! Everyone says how good he is.'

'Then why don't you use the tickets?' Jessica suggested, seeing a way out of her quandary without being involved herself. 'You and Al could go together.'

'I'm afraid that's not possible.' The light died from Miriam's pale face. 'Al's working overtime every night this week. He won't be able to get away.'

Her tone implied that she didn't think he wanted to, and Jessica felt a sharp pang of sympathy for her friend.

'But we could go together, if you like.'

Jessica knew that her doubt showed on her face.

'I wasn't going to use them——'

'Not use them?' Miriam echoed incredulously. 'But, Jess, you can't waste them. Everyone says Daniel Tyson's going to be a really big star very soon—they say he's a brilliant satirist—the thinking man's comedian.'

It was a long time since she had seen such animation in her friend's face, Jessica reflected. For some weeks now, Miriam had been quite unlike her normal bubbly self.

'What's wrong, Miriam?'

'Nothing.' The answer came too quickly, increasing Jessica's concern. 'It's just that with Al working so much I've been on my own a lot lately. We haven't been out or anywhere in weeks. I'd love to go to this show!'

How could she resist that wistful expression? It was impossible now to say that she had no intention of using the tickets, impossible to deny Miriam the chance of an evening out which she so obviously needed.

'Well, we'll go, then. We'll make a night of it, just the two of us.'

She knew she had made the right decision when she saw the smile that transformed Miriam's face.

'Just think, if he does make it big, we'll be able to say that we knew him! I never thought he'd end up on the stage—he hasn't done so in the same way as his father, perhaps, but he's in showbusiness anyway. He always seemed much more the academic type—terribly serious-minded. Didn't he get a place at university to read law?'

Jessica nodded slowly. Daniel Tyson had been the best student of the year, leaving the college with a string of exam successes and distinctions to his name. Everyone had assumed that he was destined to become a high-flyer—so why this uncharacteristic change of direction? Because, after all, being a stand-up comic touring provincial theatres was hardly the height of success.

But then, from what Miriam had said, he was rather more than a stand-up comic. A satirist was how her friend had described him, and there were very few people who could combine that sort of critical commentary with the type of popular appeal that Daniel Tyson seemed to

be attracting. If the truth were told, she was intrigued
at the prospect of finding out just what Daniel Tyson's
show was like. There was little likelihood of her meeting
the man again, she reasoned. She would be just one
among hundreds in the audience, and, with the stage
lights shining in his eyes, there was no chance of his
picking her out from the crowd.

Nevertheless, What *am* I doing here? was the thought
uppermost in Jessica's mind as she settled into her seat
beside Miriam the following night. Privately she had to
admit to having spent the past two days in a state of
constant apprehension, wondering just what she would
do if Daniel Tyson turned up in the Jester, or if she were
to run into him in the street, and she had only really
relaxed during the time between eight and ten-thirty in
the evenings, when she had known that he was on stage
at the theatre.

'Any minute now!' Miriam, who had been worryingly
subdued since they had met, whispered in her ear. Right
on cue, the house-lights dimmed.

She would be totally detached, the cool, objective ob-
server, Jessica told herself, settling back in her seat. She
would forget all about the past and concentrate on the
present, though if her past experience of stand-up comics
was anything to go by she was in for a thoroughly boring
evening. Inwardly she sighed at the prospect of a stream
of crude *double entendres*, sexist remarks, Irish jokes
and dreary mother-in-law stories.

That thought brought her up sharply. *Did* Daniel
Tyson have a mother-in-law? For reasons she couldn't
possibly account for, the idea was strangely disturbing,
like imagining herself without the Jester, as a housewife
and the mother of three children.

'Jess, I don't believe it!' Miriam hissed in her ear. 'How did Daniel Tyson turn out to be this hunk?'

Turning her gaze to the stage, Jessica considered the man who had walked out on to it, viewing him as a man instead of the insolently provoking stranger who had so infuriated her—though, even then, she had had to admit to herself that he was a singularly attractive man.

He had filled out quite a lot, she realised. As a student, Daniel Tyson had been slim to the point of thinness—and surely his hair had been lighter then, the present dark, glossy chestnut just a nondescript brown? *This* Daniel Tyson was no scrawny youth. Dressed in black shirt and trousers, with a lightweight white jacket over the top, he was all man, well-built, with broad, straight shoulders, a strong chest and long, powerful legs. The spotlights touched his hair like a caress, highlighting its rich colour and making it gleam like burnished copper.

But even at—what, twenty?—he had had a unique magnetic appeal, one that had made other, more conventionally handsome boys look almost too pretty by comparison, and the passing years had enhanced that quality, refining it from its raw ore to an exceptionally potent force. Time had been kind to Daniel Tyson, Jessica reflected. He had grown into his face, the hard-boned features that had appeared rather too harsh on a youth now fitting perfectly with the man he had become.

That was her last rational thought for some time, because from the moment Daniel began to speak, launching into a drily witty story of the problems, largely imaginary, Jessica suspected, he had encountered on his journey to Scarby, she fell under the spell of that glorious voice and listened, entranced, losing every trace of that cool, detached objectivity she had determined on just a short time before.

And, contrary to her fears, she wasn't bored for a moment, because Daniel Tyson was *very* funny, sometimes excruciatingly so. He didn't tell jokes, but instead recounted wry, pithy stories that were so true to life they were totally, believably real. But, while they were so very amusing, at the same time they showed up the idiocies and eccentricities of human beings, their blindness and prejudices in a very thought-provoking way. These stories were combined with a brilliant gift for mimicry and a deadly sense of timing that meant that, just when the audience thought they'd got the point and could rest their laughter-aching sides, he would cap the punchline with a quick, dry comment that reduced them to helpless wrecks.

Jessica's eyes were wet with laughter-induced tears by the end of the show, and she felt exhausted, wrung out like a damp dishcloth with the effort of laughing so much. But at the same time she felt refreshed and re-vitalised, better than she had for days, her mind buzzing with ideas that Daniel Tyson's comments had aroused.

'I'm worn out!' Miriam moaned as they made their way out of the auditorium, and, glancing at her, Jessica thought that she looked very different from the subdued, withdrawn woman of just two hours before. Laughter was reputed to be the best medicine, she reflected, feeling that never before had she understood that phrase so clearly.

'Me, too. I'll have to recover before we go home. Why don't we go for a drink first?'

The theatre bar was crowded, full of people from the audience, and while Miriam claimed two seats in the corner Jessica made her way to the other side of the room, resigned to a long wait before she would be served.

All around her was the buzz of conversation, the laughter Daniel Tyson had provoked still lingering in people's voices; but, as in her own mind, it was mixed with a new perspective on some of the topics he had raised. Here and there, debates were already beginning, sparked off by what they had heard.

How had Daniel Tyson, the reclusive, serious-minded student, become that consummate performer on stage tonight? He had shown no talent for comedy at college, though she could remember one occasion when he had participated in a debate organised by a member of staff to coincide with the General Election currently being held. His forceful delivery and brilliantly thought out arguments then had been mixed with flashes of the sort of dry humour he had shown tonight, winning everyone round to his point of view so that at the final vote he had achieved a landslide victory, collecting over three-quarters of the support and leaving his three opponents with only what remained scattered between them.

If she had had to hazard a guess as to what Daniel Tyson might have become if he hadn't taken up law, she would have said a politician or something similar, Jessica thought as she took a few steps nearer the bar. And certainly he had shown tonight that he could easily hold a large audience captive and entranced. She would never, ever have expected that if she saw him again it would have been like this.

Served at last, she turned with the glasses in her hand and froze suddenly, spilling some of the wine, as her eyes went to the corner where Miriam sat and she realised that her friend was not alone.

The man sitting beside her had his back towards Jessica, his face hidden. The battered leather jacket he wore was very different from the smart black and white stage outfit she had just seen, but that jacket was all too familiar after Monday night, and there was no mistaking those powerful shoulders, the glorious, burnished chestnut of his hair.

She had convinced herself she was completely safe, that there was no chance of Daniel Tyson realising she was even in the theatre—but she hadn't reckoned on him socialising with the audience afterwards.

She couldn't face him! She couldn't sit with him, couldn't even attempt to make conversation with those humiliating memories playing over and over in her head. She couldn't even bring herself to be polite to him. And the memory of her own rashly spoken words was there too. How could she meet those mocking hazel eyes, knowing that he would remember what she had said? She had seen enough of his keen, incisive mind tonight to be distinctly apprehensive about his reaction to that.

But she couldn't just stand here all night. At any moment Miriam might look up and see her—though, right now, that seemed an unlikely possibility, she reflected wryly, noting how her friend's formerly pale face now glowed with colour, her blue eyes fixed on the man beside her. As she watched she saw Daniel Tyson lean forward and take one of Miriam's hands in both his own, his face so close to hers that they were almost touching.

And this was the man who had seduced his own stepmother! A spark of fury fired in Jessica's brain as the expression on Miriam's face reminded her of the way Tracey had looked just a couple of nights earlier, when Tyson had flirted blatantly with her. Was he making a play for Miriam now? The man must be an incorrigible womaniser. He must have seen Miriam's wedding ring—

or, having seen it, had he simply decided to ignore it? Her movements brisk and her spine stiffly straight, Jessica marched over to the table.

'Oh, there you are!'

It was impossible to miss the way Miriam's colour deepened, her embarrassed movement as she snatched her hand from Tyson's on catching sight of her friend.

'I thought you'd got lost. Jess—look who's here!'

I'm well aware of who's here! Jessica declared in the privacy of her thoughts. And I wish he weren't! Irritation made her skin prickle as she forced herself to turn her head towards the man who now rose to his feet, those changeable eyes, which some trick of the light had now made a dark, mossy green, going straight to her face with what Jessica felt was a distinctly challenging look.

The gesture of courtesy wasn't lost on Jessica, though she was inclined to believe that that was all it was—a gesture. Daniel Tyson probably knew all the tricks and used them skilfully. Travelling the country as he did, playing different towns every week, it was very likely that he picked up a different woman everywhere he went. Possibly he had his own set of groupies in the way that a pop star or an actor might have. With his looks and the charisma that came from being on the stage, he could probably pick and choose, innocent, gullible girls falling into his hands like ripe plums. Well, not this girl, Mr Tyson!

'Mr Tyson.' She made the acknowledgement coolly, just a tilt of her head in his direction her only gesture, her wide grey eyes carefully indifferent.

'Hello, Mystery.'

Two words; just two words in that rich, smooth voice, but they were enough to rock Jessica's composure, making a rush of colour she couldn't control flare in her cheeks as her fingers tightened around the glasses she held. It was as if the past nine years had been stripped away so that she felt once more like a girl of eighteen, standing at the college gates with Daniel Tyson's hand on her arm, restraining her when she would have pulled away.

'I want to talk to you,' he had said, and, her pride in ruins, still smarting fiercely from the way he had humiliated her, she had flashed back,

'Well, I don't want to talk to *you*! You can have nothing to say that I might conceivably want to hear!'

'Don't be silly, Jess——'

'Jess?' Jessica's temper had boiled over. 'Don't you dare call me Jess! That's a name I only allow my friends to use! It's Miss Terry to you!'

She had wrenched her arm away from him then and escaped, trying to stalk away to express her anger and contempt for him, though the way her legs had been trembling had turned the movement into an undignified half run.

She had never wanted to see Daniel Tyson again, though of course she had had to. In the normal course of college life she was forced to meet him many times, and each time he had found some reason to address her, not as Miss Terry, but sliding the syllables of her name together to create the sardonic nickname 'Mystery'.

'Here, let me take those.'

The deep voice was solicitous, his concern apparently genuine as he eased the glasses from her clenched fingers and placed them on the table. But a gleam of amusement lurked in the depths of his eyes, aggravating her discomposure with all the unsaid things it expressed.

He had known all along! Jessica's legs were suddenly unsteady beneath her, and she slumped down into the nearest chair without a thought for dignity or elegance. He had known all the time who she was! During that confrontation in the restaurant, when she had been totally unaware of his identity, he had known only too well that she was the Jessica Terry he had known all those years ago. In the disturbed whirlpool of her thoughts, Jessica was shocked to find that mixed in with her consternation was a tiny stream of pleasure at the thought that, after all, he hadn't found her completely forgettable.

'Mr Tyson!' Miriam's voice expressed disbelief. 'Why so formal, Jess? After all, we knew each other at college. Isn't it great to see Dan again after all this time?'

Dan. Jessica registered the warmth with which Miriam had used the shortened form of Daniel Tyson's name with a *frisson* of apprehension. He had certainly used his time well in the—what?—ten minutes he had had alone with her. Seeing the sparkle in Miriam's eyes, a sparkle which had been missing for quite some time, she was strongly tempted to ignore their untouched drinks and get to her feet, declaring that it was time they left. Miriam was a married woman—normally a *happily* married woman—and Jessica herself was very fond of Al. She had no wish to see that marriage threatened because of the dubious and potentially dangerous excitement of a passing flirtation with a practised charmer like Daniel Tyson.

'As a matter of fact, Jessica and I renewed our acquaintance—on Monday. I had dinner at the Jester and we met up again there.'

'Jess!' Miriam turned a reproachful glance on her friend. 'You never told me.'

'It slipped my mind.' Jessica's tone was deliberately dismissive. 'And, besides, I didn't know who he was.'

Her gaze went to Daniel's face, cool grey eyes locking
with gleaming hazel ones. 'I didn't remember you at all.'

There was a perverse sort of pleasure in saying the
words as squashingly as possible. That should put Daniel
Tyson in his place, let him know he wasn't totally irresistible to all women.

Unfortunately, Daniel didn't look at all squashed. Instead, Jessica saw a gleam of appreciation and challenge
light in his eyes.

'I didn't think you did,' he said, holding her gaze with
his own, so that for a moment it was as if they were
enclosed in their own tiny bubble of space and time,
Miriam and the rest of the crowded room seeming to
cease to exist. 'And the conversation you were having
was so fascinating that I decided it would be much more
interesting not to disillusion you.'

Wrenching her eyes from his, Jessica reached for her
glass and took a hasty swallow of her wine. She might
have known that Daniel would not be able to resist the
opportunity to get in a dig about that. She could only
pray that he hadn't caught the earlier part of her conversation with John, knowing a swift rush of relief at
the recollection of the other man's careful whisper when
he had recounted the sordid truth about Daniel's departure from Scarby.

'You know what they say about eavesdroppers never
hearing any good of themselves,' she retorted, her mental
discomfort making her voice taut.

Daniel's slow smile did uncomfortable things to her
nerves, making them feel raw and tender, as if a piece
of sandpaper had been scraped over them.

'You could hardly call it eavesdropping. I think the
whole restaurant must have heard every word.'

His voice was low and deceptively gentle, but all the same Jessica could feel the sparks of antagonism between them so clearly that she almost expected to see them flash on the air, and she couldn't drag her gaze away from those clear, challenging hazel eyes.

'Would you two please explain what you're talking about?' Miriam put in plaintively. 'I'm lost!'

Jessica was surprised how much effort it took to direct her attention towards her friend.

'When Mr Tyson came to the restaurant on Monday, he overheard a conversation I was having with John Bennett. We were talking about stand-up comics and I——' She hesitated, unsure of how to go on.

'Had some rather critical opinions,' Daniel supplied, with an exaggerated helpfulness that had her gritting her teeth against a furious explosion.

'In general, I've found very few so-called comedians actually funny,' she flashed back. Then, angry with herself at the way she had revealed how much he was getting to her, she reined in her temper ruthlessly and continued in a coolly reasonable tone. 'So many of them seem to rely on a few tired old jokes with the same themes as the butt of their "humour", and they end up being at best thoroughly boring and at worst positively offensive.'

'But you can't say that about Dan's show,' Miriam put in. 'You were laughing as much as anyone all the way through—I heard you.'

Thanks, pal, Jessica told her silently, flicking a swift, sidelong glance in Daniel's direction, expecting to see smiling triumph on his face. Instead she was surprised by the fact that his expression was a politely listening mask, though one dark eyebrow drifted upwards questioningly when he saw the movement of her eyes.

'I was pleasantly surprised tonight,' she admitted grudgingly, and would have preferred to have left it at that, but something about that direct, challenging gaze made her reconsider her remark and see how impolite it sounded.

Her conscience pricked her painfully and innate honesty forced her to add, 'I enjoyed the show very much, Mr Tyson. It was extremely witty and—refreshingly different.'

Her voice failed her on the last word, making it come out in a shaken, uneven gasp, as for the first time she was treated to the sort of smile that had had such an effect on Tracey. She was shocked to find that she wasn't as immune to it as she would have liked to be, her breath catching in her throat and her pulse setting up an uncomfortable, jerky rhythm that made her blood pound in her ears.

Damn the man! No one had the right to be so attractive, not unless his character matched the appeal of his looks. It was strange how, in the past, painters had depicted the Devil as an ugly, repulsive creature. If she could paint, *her* Prince of Darkness would be handsome, smiling, seductive, infinitely appealing—the very image, in fact, of the man sitting opposite her.

'Thank you for the compliment.' The deep, rich tones were like a caress. 'I appreciate it, especially from someone as strongly critical as you.'

That wicked glint was back in his eyes again, mocking her, seeming to say, I hope you didn't find it too difficult to think of something nice to say. Provoked beyond endurance, Jessica couldn't bite her tongue, even though common sense told her that was the wisest thing to do.

'It wasn't a *compliment*, Mr Tyson. Compliments are often insincere, made because you think it's what the other person wants to hear and you want to please them. I simply expressed what I felt as honestly as possible.'

Not quite, her conscience reproved her. To be completely honest, she would have had to say that she hadn't enjoyed a show so much in years, that she had rarely been treated to such a display of sparkling intelligence and wit, combined with an incisive perceptiveness that had taken her breath away, so that the two hours he had been on stage had flashed past, seeming more like two minutes, and leaving her longing for more. But that was something she wasn't prepared to admit to Daniel Tyson.

'Which makes your opinion all the more valuable. Showbusiness has more than its fair share of flatterers and hangers-on who are only too prepared to say what they think you want to hear, not what they really feel. It's not easy to get a genuine objective criticism, which is why I value honesty when I hear it.'

The candid sincerity in Daniel's eyes and tone stirred the whirlpool of confusion in Jessica's mind once more, and she was unnerved to find that her hand was faintly unsteady as she raised her glass to her lips again. Had she misjudged this man? Was he not, after all, the shallow, practised flirt and showbusiness phoney she had taken him to be? That smile, that hypnotic voice, made her want to throw caution to the winds and simply enjoy being with him.

'And couldn't we make it Daniel?' he went on, a hint of cajolery sliding into his voice, making it devastatingly seductive, the sort of voice Svengali must have had. 'After all, we're not exactly strangers.'

It was so much easier and much, much more pleasant to respond to that appeal than to keep stiffly to her resolve not to be swayed by his charm, and, unable to stop herself, Jessica found that her lips were curving into a smile, her eyes losing their coolly distant look and lighting with genuine warmth.

'Daniel it is, then.'

As soon as she had made it, the concession worried her, leaving her feeling ill at ease and strangely vulnerable, so that she rushed on hastily, 'So how do you find Scarby now you've come back? Is it as you remember it?'

As she spoke, John's story, briefly forgotten, surfaced in her mind again so that she scarcely heard Daniel's reply. How could she have let that smile affect her so that she had forgotten just what sort of a man Daniel Tyson was?

'It hasn't changed much. It's a little more shabby and run-down—and, of course, places you knew when you were young always seem so much smaller when you visit them afterwards as an adult.'

Had what John had said been true or just scandal? Taking a deep breath, Jessica nerved herself to test the water.

'But of course you must have been back quite often since you left college—to visit your father.'

Immediately she knew her words had been a mistake. The heavy eyelids hooded his eyes, the small movement vividly expressive of his total withdrawal, and it was as if a cloud had passed in front of the sun as every trace of warmth faded from his face, leaving it as cold and hard as if it had been carved from granite. The contrast with the appeal of his smile only moments earlier was so intense that Jessica actually felt physically cold, a shiver of fear running down her spine.

With that easy charm stripped away, Daniel Tyson was a different man altogether, a hard, steel-eyed character whose strong-boned features and firm jaw spoke of ruthless determination and intransigent disregard for anyone who was fool enough to get in his way. Without a smile on it, that wide, mobile mouth seemed just a thin, harsh line, as unwelcoming and unyielding as the features above it.

'I haven't been back at all,' he said in a voice that, while it was perfectly polite on the surface, still managed to lace every word with an unspoken warning, so that they fell into the air like drops of ice. This topic was to be pursued no further, his tone said, and Jessica knew she would be a fool not to heed it.

But she was free to think, and every instinct told her that Daniel's reaction proved John's story had been true. With a tiny unconscious movement she edged her chair to one side, away from Daniel's, hating the thought of being so close to such a despicable character.

'Where does your tour take you after Scarby?'

It was Miriam who spoke, causing Jessica to send her a mental vote of thanks for the way she had stepped into the breach, filling the uncomfortable silence. She herself was incapable of thinking of a thing to say, because if she opened her mouth it would be to lash out at him verbally, tell him just what she thought of him—and those thoughts definitely needed censoring before they were fit to air in public.

'You're here until Saturday, and then what? Does the tour end then?'

'No such luck.' A wry smile tugged at the corners of Daniel's mouth. 'I'm in Doncaster next week, Sheffield the week after that. Then Leeds, Manchester—it'll be weeks before I hit base again.'

'And that base is where?'

'It must be very hard for you, all that travelling——'

Jessica's question and Miriam's sympathetic comment clashed, their voices speaking simultaneously, and echoes of Jessica's earlier concern resurfaced as she saw how, without hesitation, Daniel turned to Miriam to answer her first.

'It can be hard, but it's very satisfying and it can also be a lot of fun, though I have to admit that I'm getting sick and tired of hotel bedrooms. I miss my books and my records, but most of all I hate not having room to move around in—spread myself. My flat in London——'

A flicker of a glance in Jessica's direction was the only indication that he had even registered her question which he was now belatedly answering.

'—may not be Buckingham Palace, but anything beats the claustrophobia of a single hotel room night after night.'

'Don't you ever want to settle down? Marry? Have children?'

Jessica frowned as she heard the unevenness of Miriam's voice on the last question. It was time she got her friend out of here.

'Show me the woman who'd put up with the way I live.' Daniel's grin was lopsided—deliberately so, Jessica felt. He must know to an inch the appeal of that boyishly rueful expression. 'I rarely know myself where I'm going to be from one week's end to the next. It wouldn't suit a married man.'

But it suited him, Jessica reflected cynically. There hadn't been even a hint of regret in his voice. Being in a different place each week was probably just how he liked things—like a sailor, he probably had a different girl in every port of call.

'A *wife* certainly wouldn't want to sit at home waiting for you to turn up every six weeks or so,' she put in and, as she had hoped, her careful emphasis provoked a strangled squawk from Miriam.

'Al will be home! Jess—I'm sorry but I'm going to have to go. Don't let me drag you away. You don't have to give me a lift, I can get a bus.'

'Perhaps I could drive you home,' Daniel put in quickly, too quickly, Jessica thought, intensifying her suspicions about his motives where Miriam was concerned. She couldn't forget the memory of his hand linked with Miriam's, her friend's uneasy start at her arrival, the glow of pleasure in her eyes.

'There's no need for that.' She had meant her voice to sound crisply definite, instead it came out taut and snappish. 'I'm quite ready to leave myself.'

And she was—more than ready. She didn't want to spend another minute in Daniel Tyson's company.

'*I'll* take you home, Miriam,' she added hastily, wanting to forestall the protest that was clearly forming on Daniel's lips. 'It's no problem.'

'But you live on the opposite side of town to Miriam.' Infuriatingly, Daniel seemed every bit as determined as she was. 'And my hotel is only a mile away from her house. It makes much more sense for me to take her in my car.'

So he wasn't staying with his father. That wasn't exactly surprising. Melvyn Tyson would probably rather die than have his son set foot in his house again—and Jessica could hardly blame him.

A second, more worrying thought struck Jessica. How did Daniel know where she and Miriam lived? He must be a really fast worker to get so much information out of her friend in such a short time or——

A new idea stopped her thought processes dead, and it was a moment or two before her brain would function again. Had Daniel simply come to the Jester on a chance recommendation, or had he already made some enquiries about people he had known before? And if he had, why would he want to know about *her*? The answer to that question didn't come easily.

'*I'm* going to drive Miriam home,' she declared with what even she recognised as unnecessary vehemence. 'I brought her here and I'm taking her back.'

'What on earth's got into you two?'

Miriam looked totally bemused—as well she might, Jessica thought wryly. She and Daniel were like two angry terriers fighting over a bone. It was all rather foolish, but she was determined not to back down. Miriam was vulnerable at the moment; too vulnerable to be left to the not-so-tender mercies of an unfeeling womaniser like Daniel Tyson. Grey eyes flashing fire, she glared furiously at the man opposite her, but he appeared totally unmoved by her anger.

'It's much more sensible to let me do it—much more practical.'

The coldly reasonable voice incensed Jessica. Throwing caution to the winds, she rounded on him violently.

'I don't care about the practicalities! Miriam is my friend——'

And I'll defend her against you if she can't see the truth for herself, she was sorely tempted to add, but never got the chance.

'There's no need for all this! I can get a bus,' Miriam exclaimed—then, after one swift glance at their faces, seeing the determination not to give in that was stamped so clearly on both of them, she stood up in exasperation. 'Oh, sort it out between the two of you. I'm going to the Ladies.'

'I'll meet you outside, Miriam,' Daniel called after her as she moved away.

'Oh, no, you don't——' Jessica spluttered, but he was already on his feet and heading for the door, leaving her with no alternative but to follow if she was to continue this argument—which she was determined to do. Daniel Tyson wasn't getting his own way in this, not if she could help it!

'Now, look——'

Her words went unheeded; Daniel was already halfway down the stairs. Jessica followed as swiftly as she could, her movements hampered by her high heels so that she was no match for his long, easy stride that took two steps at once. Outside the main doors he stopped at last, and she was supremely conscious of those narrowed tiger's eyes on her face as, rather breathless and distinctly flurried, she came up to him.

'What's the problem, Mystery?' he drawled before she could open her mouth.

'The problem is *you*!'

The use of that mocking nickname incensed her, and that infuriating habit of lifting one eyebrow in a sardonically questioning way fanned the flames of her anger until they were blazing out of control, leaving no room for rational thought, no time to consider whether she had possibly over-reacted to his behaviour towards Miriam.

'Me?'

'Yes, you! Miriam's a married woman—she's not available—and I don't want to see her marriage put at risk by someone like you! So why don't you just leave her alone and turn your attentions to someone else?'

'You?' The single syllable stopped her dead. Silkily spoken as it was, it seemed to have the effect of a slap in the face, leaving her mind completely blank. But, as she recovered and drew breath to repudiate the suggestion furiously, Daniel continued smoothly, 'Could it be that you're jealous, Mystery?'

'Jealous?'

'You never used to be so reticent about asking for what you want, so why start now? You've only got to ask—I'd be more than ready to oblige.'

You've only got to ask? What *was* the man talking about? She wasn't given time to think. Even as her mind struggled with the problem, Daniel took a step closer, his hands going out to fasten on her arms, and the next moment she was pulled firmly against him as his mouth came down hard on hers.

CHAPTER FOUR

IF JESSICA had been hit over the head with a crowbar she couldn't have been more stunned. The ground seemed to rock beneath her feet and she clutched at Daniel's jacket to prevent herself from falling, only to realise that the action was a mistake when, clearly taking it as encouragement, he pulled her closer, his arms coming round her, encasing her in a steel grasp from which it was impossible to break free.

Her sense of outrage was like a scream in her mind, driving her to lash out with one foot in a vicious kick directed at the long, denim-clad legs so temptingly close to her own. Daniel's muffled grunt of pain was infinitely satisfying, but his reaction was quite the opposite to what she had intended. His grip didn't weaken, in fact it tightened even more, crushing her painfully, and, as if he was determined to obtain retribution for her foolish and unthinking action, his mouth covered hers again savagely.

But by now Jessica's mind was clearing, the haze of shock evaporating, and she found herself able to think more rationally. Her attempt to fight him hadn't been successful, but there was more than one way to skin this particular cat. A blow to the ego could often be as effective as any physical assault.

With a tiny, mental smile she made herself relax against Daniel, letting her lips soften against his, feeling his instinctive response as his kiss became less of a savage attack and more of a genuine caress. This was better;

this was what she wanted. If she just opened her mouth a little...

What followed was as unnerving as it was unexpected. Even while her mind was working completely rationally on one level, another, subconscious part of it suddenly seemed to awaken so that the heady thrill of triumph was mixed with another, more basic reaction, one that was overwhelmingly intoxicating. She was intensely aware of the hard, masculine strength of the body so close to hers, the rough feel of the denim shirt and the warmth of his skin beneath it, the tantalising mixture of some tangy aftershave with Daniel's own personal scent. For several endless seconds she was suspended out of time, lost in a world of sensation. She had even lifted her hands to link them round his neck when the sound of a car door slamming pierced the fog that clouded her mind, jolting her back to reality and the recollection of what she had planned.

With a deliberate movement she nestled closer, sighing deeply.

'Jack!' she murmured softly. 'Oh, Jack——'

If she had been a poisonous snake he couldn't have released her more quickly. His head came up and he almost flung her away from him, so that she stumbled and had to put out a hand to the wall for support, her gaze flying to his face, seeing the molten anger that made his eyes gleam like a wild cat's in the moonlight.

For a moment Jessica was genuinely frightened. She had achieved her aim, rid herself of his unwanted embrace, but if looks could kill she felt she should shrivel into a pile of ashes right there on the ground before him.

'You——' he began, and she flinched at the suppressed violence in his voice. But then, abruptly, his face changed, the dark anger vanishing, to be replaced by a warm smile which made Jessica blink in confusion. It was only when Miriam spoke from behind her that she realised the reason for his stunningly swift change of mood.

'There you are! Well, have you sorted out all this non-sense about who's going to take me home? Really, I don't know why you're both being so silly about it! I'm a grown woman, I can easily get home on my own.'

'But there's no need for you to do that,' Daniel put in so smoothly that Jessica could hardly believe her ears.

What had happened to the bite of anger in his voice, the taunting mockery that had been there earlier which had so infuriated her? Daniel Tyson was a far better actor than she had ever imagined. Perhaps he took after his father in that. Certainly, if he hadn't turned to comedy, he could well have made a success of a con-ventional stage career.

'We've talked it out. Jessica didn't want to put me to any trouble, but I've convinced her that I don't mind at all—in fact, it'll be a pleasure—and so she's quite happy for me to give you a lift.' His eyes slid to Jessica's face, a gleam of amusement lighting in them as he saw her dumbfounded expression. 'That's right, isn't it?'

Jessica could only nod silently. Her voice seemed to have failed her, and even if she could have spoken she doubted if she could have formed any coherent thoughts to express.

It was shock, she told herself, shock and sheer blind fury at his unwanted assault on her to which reaction was now setting in. But, deep down, she knew that the answer wasn't as simple as that. Her own reaction to his kiss, brief as it had been, had thrown her completely off balance, and confusion and a strong reluctance to probe too deeply into things she wasn't at all sure she wanted to know about or understand kept her silent as Miriam said goodnight, though the smile on her friend's face and the way she linked her arm through Daniel's revived all her suspicions and anxieties, making her stomach twist into tight, painful knots.

'I'll see you tomorrow, Jess.'

'And I hope I will, too,' Daniel put in, once more the suave, relaxed charmer. 'It's been a—pleasure——' the word was loaded with irony '—meeting you again. I'd like to continue our conversation some time soon.'

If I never see you again it'll be too soon! Jessica wanted to shout, but the words wouldn't come, and she could only stand silently watching as Daniel led Miriam towards his car.

Conversation! That hadn't been a conversation, it had been a full-blown assault! She never in her life wanted to see Daniel Tyson again—and yet——

Jessica shook her head furiously. She didn't want to think of any 'and yet', but her mind could not erase the memory of how it had felt for those few short seconds when she had forgotten who Daniel was, and her own fears for Miriam, and had simply experienced a rush of feeling such as she had never known before in her life. In that brief space of time she had been intensely aware of Daniel as a man and herself as a woman, and her body still glowed just to recall the sensations that had flooded through her. It had started out as an act, but somewhere along the line the act had been buried under—under what?

Desire. The word came as a relief, satisfying in its lack of emotional overtones. Desire was not a rational thing and—face facts, she told herself—Daniel Tyson was a a singularly attractive male. Whatever her personal feelings about him, there was no denying that. She had experienced the potent force of his sexuality years ago—to her cost.

But Jack was an equally attractive man, an unwanted, insidious little voice whispered inside her head. And, good-looking as he was, *he* hadn't been able to light the spark that, even in anger, Daniel Tyson created so easily.

Oh, *damn* Daniel Tyson! Jessica stamped her foot hard, needing to express her muddled feelings physically. Only three days ago she had been in control of her life—a little restless, perhaps, but that could be put down to the time of year and Jack's abrupt departure. Now she felt like a boat that had had its sails and rudder smashed in a storm, floating lost and directionless on a wild, uncharted sea. She didn't even know what to think about Miriam, unable to decide if her fears had been justified or unfounded. Her friend loved Al, she was sure of that, but the marriage was going through a sticky patch—and wasn't it possible that the attentions of a character like Daniel Tyson could turn any woman's head? They had his stepmother's, she thought grimly.

Oh, it was no good, she was too tired and confused to think about it any more, and she was achieving nothing by standing here in the cold and dark; already her feet felt like blocks of ice. But the one thing that was clear in her mind as she turned and headed for her car was that, whatever Miriam felt or didn't feel, as far as Daniel Tyson was concerned, she didn't trust his motives as far as she could throw them.

It was hard to face Miriam the following morning, hard to see the way a smile curved her mouth and she set about her work with an enthusiasm that had been lacking for some weeks. Jessica had to bite her lip hard against the temptation to enquire too closely into what had happened after she and Daniel had left the previous night, especially when the few things Miriam did let slip were not at all conducive to her peace of mind.

'Dan's a lovely man, Jess—so understanding. I found him really easy to talk to.'

Jessica managed an inarticulate murmur that might have been agreement, assuming an intense interest in the food order she was working on.

'It's such a pity he's only here for a week—three more days, really. I'd like to see much more of him. He said he'd call round today and take me out to lunch.'

'Is that wise?' It was impossible to keep the sharp note of worry out of her voice. 'What would Al think?'

'Al?' The glow had faded from Miriam's face. 'I'm not at all sure what Al thinks about anything any more. He was in bed and asleep by the time I got back last night, and he didn't even wake up when Dan came in for coffee.'

So Daniel Tyson had wormed his way into the house, Jessica thought grimly, the information increasing her suspicions by one hundred per cent at a stroke. She couldn't just stand by and watch Miriam's marriage disintegrate, something she knew Miriam would regret desperately when the fantasy world of lunches with Daniel Tyson faded. She had to do something—but what?

She was no closer to an answer when twelve-thirty brought Daniel Tyson to the Jester. Jessica felt a flare of unreasoning anger as she saw the way he sauntered into the restaurant as if he owned the place, the bright chestnut hair gleaming above the now-familiar leather jacket worn with an oatmeal coloured shirt and dark beige cord trousers. The smile he turned on Tracey was that devastatingly charming one that had Jessica gritting her teeth as she recalled how, in some long-ago television interview, she had seen his father use just such a smile frequently and with careful effect to entrance the female interviewer.

That charm was as phoney as could be, a carefully assumed act, she thought wryly, her irritation fanned by the remembrance of the way, briefly, she too had fallen under the spell Daniel Tyson could weave so easily—just as Tracey was doing now. Though, if she were honest, she had to admit that that wasn't really so very surprising. With his hair tousled by the wind and with the glow the cold air had brought to his cheeks, his eyes sparkling golden brown, Daniel looked vitally alive, his confident movements, the aura of glamour that came from his place in the world of showbusiness, adding to the impact of the purely physical appeal.

Jessica felt herself bristling like an angry cat, resenting his intrusion into her own private territory. His size and strength seemed threatening and alien in the cool elegance of the restaurant's green and white décor.

'Can I help you, Mr Tyson?'

Those tiger's eyes regarded her steadily, apparently lazily good-humoured under their heavy lids, but Jessica refused to let herself be taken in by that pretence of warmth. Where Daniel Tyson was concerned, appearances were very deceptive.

'I thought we agreed on Daniel.'

During the night Jessica had convinced herself that she had exaggerated the appeal of that voice, but now she felt it begin to weave its enchantment once again so that she had to give herself a small mental shake to break the spell. He could make a fortune doing voice-overs in advertising, she thought. Those seductive tones could sell an igloo in the Sahara.

'So we did,' she managed tightly, struggling with a memory of Miriam's voice saying 'Dan', and just for a split second she knew an inexplicable longing to be able to do the same.

'I've come to collect Miriam. I'm taking her out to lunch.'

'Really?' Jessica deliberately injected a note of surprise into her voice. She wasn't going to boost this man's already over-inflated ego by letting him know that Miriam had told her about the date almost first thing that morning. 'She never mentioned it.'

She had forgotten about Tracey's presence, and now she cursed the other girl's transparent look of surprise that betrayed the lie for what it was. The muscles at the corners of Daniel's wide mouth twitched, though whether in amusement or anger Jessica was unable to judge.

'Didn't she?'

That wonderful voice was just a silky drawl. Jessica could just imagine that that was the way Shere Khan, the tiger in *The Jungle Book* might speak. A sensation like the trickle of cold water ran down her spine, making her shiver. Lazily indolent in the sun, a tiger might look like an overgrown pussycat, but when provoked it could be terrifyingly savage. Was she going to abandon Miriam, innocent and unprotected, to this particular jungle cat?

'I'm afraid Miriam's busy. We——'

'No, I'm not.' Miriam's voice broke in on her, making Jessica swing round to see her friend standing in the doorway, her coat on and her bag in her hand. Oh, Miriam, Jessica thought. Do you have to make it so obvious you can't wait? 'Everything's in hand and that delivery's not due until two, so I can take my lunch now.'

The curve at the corners of Daniel's mouth deepened into a wide smile that Jessica detested because of its evident amused triumph. She wanted to catch hold of

Miriam's hand, beg her not to go, to remember Al, but with Tracey's interest already aroused by her uncharacteristic untruthfulness a few moments before she had to content herself by saying, 'Well, make sure you're back in good time. I need to go over the arrangements for the Jenison party with you.'

'I'll be back,' Miriam assured her blithely, already heading for the door. Daniel made a move to follow her, then turned back.

'I'll make sure she comes to no harm,' he said, the dry note in his voice making it embarrassingly clear that he was well aware of what she had been trying to do. 'She'll be quite safe with me.'

If only she could believe that! The truth was that John's story had convinced her of the exact opposite, Jessica reflected unhappily as she watched Miriam and Daniel walk down the street, a sour, bitter taste coming into her mouth as she saw the way Daniel slung an arm around Miriam's shoulders, drawing her close to him. Things had gone quite far enough! She was going to do something about this the first chance she got!

Her opportunity came when Miriam returned to the restaurant, Daniel still at her side. The expected delivery of fruit and vegetables had arrived early, and there was some query that only Miriam, who had phoned through the order, could help clear up. As her friend reluctantly bade Daniel a hasty goodbye and hurried off to deal with the problem, Jessica stepped forward.

'I'd like a word with you, Daniel,' she said, keeping her tone carefully neutral and using his name deliberately. There was no need to arouse his suspicions or— she thought with a faint shiver—his antagonism too soon. 'Have you got a minute?'

'Sure.' His response came surprisingly easily. 'I'm not due at the theatre until six, so I've got all afternoon.'

Jessica sincerely hoped it wouldn't take that long, but, recalling how his face had changed when she had spoken of his father, the dark, implacable side to Daniel Tyson she had seen then, she found that a sensation like the quivering of a thousand butterfly wings started up in her stomach, so that it was a struggle to keep her voice even.

'We'll go into my office. We can sit down there.'

She'd feel more confident behind her desk, with the expanse of wood between her and Daniel, and hope-fully, sitting down, he wouldn't seem quite so imposing. Even though there was so little difference in their height, standing here like this, she was far too aware of the size and breadth of him, the solid bulk of his chest, the power of his hard body, for comfort.

But even the carefully planned distance did nothing to diminish the impact of that burnished copper hair and those glowing amber eyes as Daniel settled himself into a chair, lounging back with an ease that she was very far from feeling, and stretching his long legs out in front of him, crossing them at the ankles.

'So what did you want to talk about?'

It was one thing to resolve to have this out with him, quite another to launch straight into it with that dis-turbingly keen gaze fixed on her face.

'Would you like some coffee? I could——'

'Not for me, thanks.' Daniel smoothly cut off that line of retreat. Asking Tracey to bring them a tray of coffee, pouring it out, would have given her some much-needed time to think. 'I had a very large lunch, remember.'

'Where did you go?'

The slight twist to his mouth revealed that he recognised her diversionary tactics for what they were, and despised her for resorting to them, but he answered easily enough.

'The George. Miriam chose it.'

'Oh, yes. I've heard it's very pleasant there.'

Jessica straightened some papers quite unnecessarily, put a pencil back into the holder on her desk-top, unable to meet his eyes. Making polite, trivial conversation was stupid, but she just didn't know how to begin.

'Come on, Mystery, let's have it!' Impatience sharpened Daniel's tone. 'It's obvious that something's bugging you, so why don't you just come right out and say what it is?'

'I——'

Jessica smoothed nervous hands over the skirt of her grey linen suit, then immediately wished she hadn't as she saw Daniel's eyes flick downwards to follow the movement, his gaze resting on her slim legs in the sheer grey tights, a slow smile of sensual appreciation curving his lips. With an abrupt movement she swung slightly to her right so that her legs were under the desk, pulling her chair up closer jerkily. The man was incorrigible! Did he flirt with anything in a skirt? The memory of Tracey's face made her reflect that probably the answer to that was 'yes', and irritation combined with her unease to make her rush into unguarded speech.

'Just what is going on between you and Miriam?'

That single eyebrow quirking upwards was meant to be deliberately provoking, she was sure.

'Going on?'

'Don't pretend you don't know what I mean! Miriam's a married woman——'

'I know—you made a point of telling me.'

'A *happily* married woman!' Jessica struggled to ignore the sardonic interjection.

'Do you really think so?'

'Oh, I know things aren't perfect at the moment——'

How had this happened? She had started out with the intention of questioning him, but now the tables seemed to have been turned, and Daniel was the one grilling *her*!

'But that's only temporary. Al's been working so hard—everyone goes through phases when things aren't right, but they usually work things out. But it doesn't help if someone interferes, flirts with one of the partners for their own selfish ends.'

'Is that what you think I'm doing?'

The question came with such a sharp intensity that the force of it almost rocked Jessica back in her seat, her mind reeling as she met the impact of those tiger's eyes head on. What was behind his words? Was he trying to say that Miriam meant more to him than that? Surely he wasn't trying to claim that he'd fallen in love with her? They hadn't known each other as adults for more than a day!

To her complete consternation, the thought of Daniel Tyson falling in love with Miriam—with anyone—shattered her already precarious composure.

'*Is it?*' The two words were laced with a cold anger that seemed to sear her nerves like the burn of acid.

'What am I to think?' she hedged uneasily. 'What *is* Miriam to you?'

'What has she told you?' Daniel countered her question with one of his own.

'Nothing. Just that you took her home—and that you'd arranged lunch today.'

She hated the smile that crossed the wide mouth, knowing it came from a sense of triumph at having caught her out in the lie she had told him earlier when she had said that Miriam hadn't mentioned their lunch date.

'I think anything else had better come from Miriam herself. Why don't you ask her?'

Because Miriam wasn't the one making all the moves. Because if Daniel Tyson hadn't singled her out, hadn't concentrated his all-too-persuasive charm on her, she would never, ever have looked at another man, Jessica was sure of that.

'I'm asking you. Just what is going on?'

'What business is it of yours?'

'Miriam's my friend——'

'I could say the same, too. And friends——'

'*Friends?*' Jessica queried with a cynical laugh. 'We were never friends, Daniel Tyson!'

Her eyes skittered away from his, not wanting to see his expression, knowing only too well the memories he must inevitably be recalling.

'You went your own sweet way, and to hell with anyone else, just as——'

She broke off abruptly, swallowing hard as Daniel suddenly sat forward in his chair, the indolent ease replaced by a tension that made her think unnervingly of the tiger she had seen in him poised ready to spring.

'As I do now?' The darkly sardonic tone did nothing to ease her racing pulse, which was already beating in an uncomfortable, jerky rhythm. 'That was what you were about to say, wasn't it?'

It was impossible to deny it. Recalling his academic success, the glittering career everyone believed he had ahead of him, it didn't indicate a consistent, hard-

working personality to have thrown everything up for
the spurious glory of the world of showbusiness.

An image of the younger Daniel Tyson slid into her
mind, that harsh-boned face much thinner, all planes
and angles. *How* had that serious, industrious student
become the man who now sat opposite her? Had he
envied his father his fame and wanted some of it for
himself? If he had, he certainly hadn't matched his
father's success. Brilliant as his show had been—and
innate honesty forced her to admit that brilliant was the
only way to describe it—he was still touring provincial
theatres at an age when Melvyn Tyson had already been
a star.

'You're only here for a week,' she said, sidestepping
the issue awkwardly. 'If you can't manage without female
company for that long, I'm sure you can find someone
else who'd be only too willing to help you while away
the long, lonely hours when you're not on stage. Why
Miriam? There must be hundreds of other girls——'

'Hundreds?'

That wry, slightly self-derogatory smile had a disturbing effect. In anyone else, Jessica would have found
it very appealing, and the way it gave the hard-featured
face a boyish vulnerability tugged at something deep
inside her.

'That's very flattering, Jessica, but I'm afraid it's
something of an exaggeration.'

After that satirical 'Mystery', the sound of her own
name spoken in that beautiful voice had a warmly attractive note that Jessica had to struggle to ignore, but
the glow that flooded through her was very soon cooled
by Daniel's next words.

'But if you're so concerned about my lack of female companionship, you could always do something about it.'

'Do——!' Hastily Jessica converted the shocked exclamation into a careful question. 'Do what?'

'You could always take Miriam's place.'

'You can't mean that!'

She couldn't believe that this was happening. She had intended to warn him off, make him see that his attentions towards Miriam were a bad idea, appeal to his better nature—if he had one—so that he would end the affair before it really began, before Miriam became deeply involved, risking being badly hurt. Instead, she found herself on the receiving end of an invitation that was the last thing she wanted.

'Not on your life! I wouldn't——'

Her voice failed her as his shoulders lifted in an offhand shrug.

'Fair enough.' His tone was nonchalant, dismissive. 'I have two more days in Scarby—I planned to use one of those to drive out into the country and I intend to have some company on the trip. It's your day off tomorrow, Miriam's on Saturday. The choice is yours.'

'Choice?'

Jessica cursed the way her dry throat turned her voice into a hoarse croak. She had been unnerved by the confident way he had mentioned her day off. She might have expected that he would have found out that Miriam wouldn't be working on Saturday—and that Al would, she added with a private pang of concern—but why should he have bothered to find out when *her* day off was? The idea of him prying into her life was infinitely distasteful.

'Between you and Miriam.' Daniel's smile was easy, infuriatingly so, Jessica thought, her tension aggravated by the way he seemed so totally in control when she was as unsettled as some small animal that sensed a predator nearby. 'I've promised myself this day out—and part of the enjoyment for me will be to have some attractive woman with me. If you don't want to come, fine—I'll ask Miriam instead.'

'You——'

Twice Jessica tried to complete the sentence, but both times her voice failed her so that she felt she must look like a stranded fish, floundering with her mouth wide open, the ridiculous image severely damaging to her self-esteem.

'It doesn't matter to me which one of you comes,' Daniel continued imperturbably. 'But I'm determined it will be one of you. So tell me, Mystery, which one will it be? You?'

'Never!' That hateful nickname provoked her into speech at last.

'OK.' Another shrug lifted those broad shoulders. 'Then Miriam will be the one.' He made a move to get to his feet. 'I'll go and make the arrangements now.'

The slight movement spurred Jessica into action. She no longer feared she might be over-reacting. Daniel Tyson was clearly determined to flirt with Miriam and to hell with the consequences, and it was equally clear that her own comments about her friend's marriage had had no effect—so much for appealing to his better nature! She couldn't sit back and let him take Miriam out for the whole day. Her stomach clenched in apprehension at the thought of the effect that might have, particularly with Miriam in her present vulnerable state of mind.

'Wait!'

But beyond that single word she could progress no further. She would do anything to stop Miriam getting involved with this man—*anything*, she repeated forcefully—but the only alternative offered was that she should spend the day with Daniel herself, and her mind rebelled at the thought.

'Yes, Mystery?'

The deceptively mild enquiry was belied by the probing force of his gaze. Damn the man! He knew exactly where he had her—in a corner, with her back up against the wall—and—*damn* him!—he was thoroughly enjoying that fact.

'I don't want to go anywhere with you!'

'Fair enough.' His total impassivity was even more galling than his earlier provocation, and it had Jessica gritting her teeth against the furious outburst she was tempted to fling at his lazily smiling face. 'As I've said, it doesn't matter to me one way or the other.'

But it did matter to Miriam. Jessica pictured her friend as she'd seen her on her wedding day, a girl with stars in her eyes. She had looked as if all her dreams had come true, which, for her, they had. She had known Al since she was sixteen, they had been true childhood sweethearts, apparently destined to live happily ever after with the large family that both Miriam and her husband longed for. So was she going to let one day spent in this man's uncomfortable company—eight hours at most— threaten that?

'Where—exactly do you intend to go?' She couldn't suppress her innermost feelings firmly enough to make her words sound anything other than grudging and reluctant.

'I thought I might visit a few old haunts, but mainly I want to get in a walk on the moors. I've missed them since I went to London, missed the freedom, the space, the wind in my hair——'

Well, that at least was something Jessica could sympathise with. Since opening the Jester she had had very little time to herself, and just lately what free time she'd had had been spent with Jack. Jack regarded the moors as wild, alien terrain. He had shuddered at the thought of tramping across them for hours, concerned at the thought of possible damage to his elegant shoes, mud-stains on his immaculate trousers. Only now did Jessica realise how she had been driven to being a city person, tied to the streets, the nightclubs and bars which formed the backbone of Jack's social life. A wave of longing for the freedom Daniel had described swept over her, and she smoothed a restless hand over her sleek mane of blonde hair. A walk on the moors would be pure heaven—but heaven tainted by the presence of Daniel Tyson, like the serpent in the Garden of Eden.

'Did you plan to make a day of it?'

Those changeable eyes were slightly narrowed, emphasising that heavy-lidded, sensual look.

'I have to be at the theatre by six, but until then, yes. I thought I'd leave early, have lunch in a pub somewhere——'

He stopped abruptly as he noticed her tiny, unconscious nod of agreement. She couldn't help herself, the plan sounded very appealing—but was it appealing enough to make her forget who she would be with?

'Why the concern for my plans, Jessica? I thought you weren't interested.'

'I didn't say that.' She caught his sceptical glance and hastily amended her declaration. 'I can change my mind, can't I?'

Daniel inclined his head slightly as if considering, his eyes coldly assessing, in a way that made her feel as if her skin had been scraped raw where they rested on her face.

'That's a woman's prerogative,' he drawled lazily. 'But if this is your way of saying you want to come with me, you've lost your chance. I gave you first option and you refused it.'

He paused meaningfully, and in the silence Jessica could hear her own voice declaring, 'I don't want to go anywhere with you!' The echo of her cold, hard words made her wince mentally.

'So, now it's Miriam's turn. I'm sure she'll be much more amenable.'

'But——'

The rush of confused emotions that flooded through Jessica brought a betraying colour to her cheeks. Her determination to protect Miriam from Daniel's attentions warred with her dislike of this arrogant male, a man who had no respect for conventional morality, who had seduced his own stepmother and was now apparently totally indifferent to Miriam's married state. The resulting volatile mixture was aggravated by the fact that now, when it seemed out of reach, she realised how much she wanted that expedition to the moors. It was as if Daniel's words had unlocked a door in her mind, one that had previously been kept firmly shut, and all the longings that had been hidden behind it had poured out with the force of a tidal wave.

'But I want to come! I'd like to! It's years since I was out on the moors.'

Just for a second something flickered in his eyes, as if he had been taken aback by her vehemence—as she had been herself, Jessica reflected, frankly stunned by her outburst. For a long, taut moment there was silence, then Daniel got to his feet and stretched lazily.

'Then go on your own—or get Jack the Lad to take you.' There was a new coldness about his face, one that turned his eyes to hard, golden pebbles.

So her use of Jack's name last night had stung, catching him on the raw. Was that what all this was about—revenge for that blow to his ego? Couldn't he bear to think that there was any woman who might be immune to his charms, someone who preferred another man to him? And where did that leave Miriam? Was Daniel Tyson just using her?

A tiny thread of rational thought reminded Jessica that her fears for Miriam were based on very little evidence. She knew nothing about Daniel, who was now a very different man from the youth she had once known. So he had held Miriam's hand, had insisted on taking her home, but wasn't she jumping to conclusions based on her own prejudice against Daniel as a result of that long-ago humiliation at his hands?

That thought drew her eyes to the strong-fingered hands now resting lightly on Daniel's narrow hips, and she shivered involuntarily at the memory of them touching her, drawing a response from her body that had been like a nuclear explosion in her mind.

'You've got your own car, Mystery—you can go any-where you want. Miriam is dependent on her husband, and right now...'

The rest of his words faded as the image of Miriam's expression when she had spoken of Daniel that morning surfaced in Jessica's mind. She hadn't been imagining the glow about the other woman's eyes, the smile that lit her face—and she hadn't imagined John's story of Daniel being found in bed with his father's wife. She didn't know what Daniel Tyson planned—though she feared the worst—but she could guess how her friend was feeling—and that smile spelt danger to Miriam's marriage.

'Yes, I've got a car, but a walk on the moors alone is no fun...'

Her voice trailed off as Daniel moved, coming close to her and leaning against her desk, those powerful, square-tipped fingers resting on its polished surface.

'If you want to come, Mystery, you'll have to ask.'

'I——'

Jessica swallowed hard against the sour taste in her mouth. He had taken things too far. She couldn't do this—it was too distasteful, too humiliating—and yet, for Miriam's sake, she had to do something.

'I'd really like to go with you,' she managed, her stomach clenching nervously as she saw the way he shook his head, that wide mouth set in an adamant line.

'Not good enough. You can do better than that—much better——'

He leaned towards her, the scent of his body reaching her nostrils in a way that sent a shivering sense of awareness shooting through her, drying her mouth so that she wetted her lips uneasily with her tongue, her breath catching in her throat as she saw those hazel eyes flick downwards to follow the tiny movement.

'You know what to do, Jessica, you've done it before.' Daniel's beautiful voice was low and husky, the hypnotic, seductive quality in it drawing her eyes to his and holding them mesmerised. 'Remember, I know just how you ask for something when you really want it.'

He was so close now that she could feel the warmth
of his body against her skin, hear the regular beat of
his heart, see his chest rise and fall softly as he breathed.
She wanted desperately to move away but she couldn't;
she found herself frozen, as if some invisible force held
her transfixed while her mind went back over the years,
remembering...

Had she really behaved like that? Had she pushed
herself on to him, insinuating her body close up against
his—against that firm chest, those strong thighs—using
her adolescent sexuality quite blatantly, running her
hands through his hair, pressing kisses on the strong
column of his neck—and all because she couldn't bear
to take second place, let someone else be Queen Bee.
Had she really been so stupid, so arrogant? She felt sick
at the thought.

'What's the matter, Mystery?' The silky voice goaded
softly. 'Lost your touch? Or could it be that, after all,
you don't want this quite so much?'

Brusquely Jessica turned her head away, her mind in
turmoil. She *did* want it—and for far less selfish reasons
than nine years before. She wanted to distract him from
Miriam far more than she had wanted his attention all
that time ago. What she aimed for now was infinitely
more important than that salve to her foolish adolescent
pride, so why couldn't she do it? Why couldn't she give
him the kiss he was angling for? It wouldn't mean anything; it was just the pressure of one pair of lips against
another, no emotion involved. It was just a kiss.

But, recalling the effect of 'just a kiss' the previous
night, she knew why she was unable to move. Deep down
inside her a new and disturbing emotion uncoiled itself,
making her nerves quiver in reaction as she recognised
it as fear. She was afraid of laying herself open to her

feelings, to the desire that had woken in her when Daniel had kissed her before. For those few, brief moments she had been out of control, not herself at all, and that wasn't something she was used to feeling. The possible implications for herself about feeling that way for a man who had shown himself to be totally indifferent to anyone else's feelings, even his own father's, made her flesh creep.

Her tongue moved nervously over dry lips once more. 'Please...'

She turned her head again, to find his face disturbingly only inches away from her own, his eyes no longer golden but a deep, dark brown that made her think of the shade of forest trees in the autumn.

'I——' Her voice croaked, broke, and she had to swallow hard. 'Daniel, please...'

'Daniel, please,' Daniel mimicked softly. 'Please what, Jessica? Please yes, or please no?'

One long finger slid under her chin, lifting her face towards his very gently.

'Is it so very hard to do?' That huskily enticing voice held her entranced, unable to move or think. 'Is this so difficult?' The brush of his lips on her cheek was like the touch of a feather. 'Or this?'

His mouth covered hers softly, delicately; feeling its gentleness, Jessica sensed the tension drain from her like air escaping from a pricked balloon. This she could handle, she thought vaguely, relaxing into the warm glow that soothed her taut muscles, smoothed away the strain she had been feeling. She didn't even worry when, leaning back, she came up against the hard strength of Daniel's arms around her, holding her close as, unconsciously, she let her mouth soften under his, allowing him to deepen and prolong the kiss.

His hands moved over her body in subtle, delicate caresses that brought a wonderful sense of relaxation in their wake. Her mind was slipping out of focus, the languorous haze that enclosed her making her limbs feel heavy. Her whole body seemed to have melted into a languid softness, so that she felt as if she were floating in a warm, sunbathed sea, limp with delight and total abandonment to pleasure. When Daniel's lips left hers, all she could manage was a faint, wordless murmur of protest.

'You've been practising.'

The coolly cynical words were like the splash of icy water in her face, jolting her back to awareness with a jarring suddenness that had her blinking in shock and confusion.

'That was not at all what I expected—very different from your previous technique. But, all in all, I think I preferred it—it was much more subtle.'

'Why, you——!'

Angry, disorientated and totally devastated, Jessica wrenched herself from his arms and sprang to her feet, her grey eyes wide above hotly burning cheeks.

'You——!'

'Relax, Mystery.' That mocking smile tormented her. 'You asked very nicely. How could I refuse you anything? I'm afraid poor Miriam will have to be disappointed.'

In a lithe, easy movement he slid from the desk and turned towards the door, then paused and looked back at Jessica, still standing bemused and speechless.

'I'll pick you up about ten tomorrow—and make sure you wear something warm and comfortable. It can get very cold on the moors at this time of year.'

Before she could gather the shattered threads of her composure together to find any words to answer him he had gone, and as Jessica watched the door swing to behind him she found that she was trembling all over with reaction.

'Very different from your previous technique... much more subtle.' Daniel's words echoed over and over in her mind until she shook her head violently in a vain attempt to try to drive them away. *Her technique?* She hadn't done anything! It was Daniel who, skilfully and seductively, had woven his spell around her so that she hadn't even noticed it was happening. *Subtle?* That wasn't the word she would have used. 'Guileful', 'cunning', 'insidious' were the adjectives that sprang to mind.

She had expected a full-blooded assault like the one he had subjected her to on the previous night, and had been totally lulled into a false sense of security by his gentle approach.

Jessica shivered, folding her arms around her body as a cold, nagging ache started up inside her. She felt lost, vulnerable, and very, very worried. Because the ache she sensed was one of loss, of frustrated longing, the result of the ruthless suppression of desire. Gentle or rough, subtle or blatant, what did it matter? Daniel had only to touch her, it seemed, and she was in out of her depth, the warm waters of sensuality closing over her head, threatening to drown all sensible or rational thought— and she had committed herself to spending the whole day with him tomorrow!

She couldn't go through with it! She *wouldn't* go through with it! But she had to—for Miriam's sake. With a sigh she faced the fact that she had no alternative but to go, though her stomach muscles twisted into tight, painful knots of apprehension at the thought.

CHAPTER FIVE

'YOU surprise me.'

Daniel paused half-way up a particularly steep climb to turn and look at Jessica toiling up the slope behind him.

'I never thought you'd last this long without whining to go back to the car.'

'When you said a walk on the moors, I assumed you meant just that!'

Jessica wished she had the strength to say more, but the effort of trudging up the hill in the wake of Daniel's long, powerful stride compelled her to keep her response short and, she hoped, pithy. She had known from the start that her attitude and appearance hadn't been quite what Daniel had expected. The way his eyes had narrowed swiftly as he took in her jade padded jacket, elderly denim jeans and sturdy, comfortable walking shoes had been more revealing than his dry question, 'Whatever happened to the sleekly elegant Miss Terry?'

Was that how he saw her? Jessica had been uncertain whether the drawled words were a compliment or not.

'My work clothes would hardly be appropriate for the sort of day you have in mind!' she retorted tightly, her voice sharpened by the disconcerting realisation that when it came down to it she had little idea as to just what sort of a day he did have in mind.

She was only too well aware of the fact that Daniel's invitation had been offered simply as an act of provocation, to test her loyalty to Miriam and to prove his power over her because of that. There was no likelihood at all that any idea of enjoying her company or making sure that she enjoyed his had ever entered his thoughts, which didn't make for a comfortable frame of mind now that ten o'clock had come round and Daniel was actually on her doorstep. Her unease was painfully aggravated by the fact that only now did she become aware of just how tightly the worn denim clung to her curving hips and legs, something which the appreciative gleam in Daniel's light eyes revealed only too clearly that he had noticed—and approved of.

Still, if there was one small comfort she could draw from all this, it was the fact that his complete indifference to which woman—herself or Miriam—accompanied him on his expedition proved that, as she had expected, his attitude towards her friend was simply that of an inveterate flirt, with no serious intent at all. That being so, if she could just distract him today and, hopefully, tomorrow, he would be on his way to Doncaster, and the worst Miriam would suffer would be the small loss of his company. There hadn't been time for her to get seriously involved.

Today was accounted for, but if she was to keep Daniel and Miriam apart on Saturday—which would be tricky because, as Daniel already knew, it was Miriam's day off, and Al would once again be working overtime—she had to ensure that he lost some of that indifference and, for the time being at least, turned his attentions towards her.

So, in spite of the effort it cost her, she set herself to being relaxed and friendly, chatting apparently easily about the places they passed, all of them well-known to her from a childhood spent growing up in Scarby.

It was surprisingly easy to do. Daniel was a good listener with an instinctive awareness of when to keep quiet and when to put in a question or a comment in order to keep the conversation going, drawing memories and stories from her with an unexpected facility. He was noticeably reticent about his own past and connections with the town which, Jessica reflected cynically, was hardly surprising. He must find it awkward to say the least to be in the same town as his father after what had happened between them.

When they abandoned the car and took to the moors Jessica found that all her old delight at tramping across the springy grass revived with a rush. The cold blast of the wind in her face was invigorating, making her cheeks glow with colour and putting a sparkle in her eyes that was intensified by her delight in the freedom of the open spaces. She had thought that Daniel shared her pleasure too, their animosity forgotten for a time, so it had come as a stinging shock to hear the sardonic comment which brought her up hard against all she had pushed to the back of her mind—and the real reason why she was here at all.

'I never thought of you as an outdoors sort of girl. You certainly never gave that impression when I—knew you before.'

Was there a note of apology, a hint of an attempt at reconciliation in his voice? That dig about the past made it unlikely, and Jessica drew a deep breath in order to retaliate.

'As I've pointed out already, we didn't exactly *know* each other—we just went to the same college—and you were there for less than a year. That hardly gives you the right to claim to be an expert on my character.'

Or for her to claim to know *his*, honesty forced her to admit, the thought disturbing her concentration on the treacherous slope so that she missed her footing and stumbled awkwardly.

'Here——' Daniel held out a hand warmly encased in a black leather glove. 'This bit *is* tough,' he went on as Jessica hesitated, pride and a lingering touch of irritation warring with a desire to accept his offer of help. She was tired, they had been walking for hours, and the slope was very steep. 'But, believe me, the view's worth it when you get to the top.'

Allowing her no chance to consider further, he gripped her hand firmly and set off again, pulling her up behind him. The strength of his grasp transmitted itself to Jessica, even through two layers of gloves, with a force that stunned her with its intensity. She was vividly aware of the power of the muscles in his hand and arm, her instinctive response making her wonder what it would feel like to have his fingers close round hers without the layers of wool and leather between them, warm skin against skin, coming together in a gesture of friendship, affection; or to have those arms hold her, not in the brutal way they had held her outside the theatre, but gently, sensually...

The last few yards of the climb passed in a hazy blur, and before she quite knew it she was standing at the top of the hill, gazing out at the countryside spread below her.

'You were right—it is—spectacular.'

She prayed that he believed her breathlessness to be the result of the effort of the climb, that it would give him no hint of the disturbed state of her feelings. She was hypersensitive to the fact that he hadn't released his grip on her hand but still held it, though more loosely now. The worrying fact was that she didn't want to pull away, but was content to let her hand rest in his, letting this moment of sharing continue for a little while at least.

Daniel's eyes were on the patchwork of fields and heather-covered moors spread before them, and she surreptitiously let her eyes slide to his face, seeing the hard-boned profile etched against the clear blue sky that was in sharp contrast to the dreary, grey, snow-laden clouds of the past few days.

He really was the most devastatingly attractive man, she thought, feeling as if she was suddenly seeing him with totally new eyes, her heightened sensitivity to his presence giving the strong planes of his features, the rich colour of his hair, the firm, determined jaw a whole new impact that shook the foundations on which her opinions of him were built. Why hadn't she noticed the warm curve to his mouth before, the laughter-lines around his eyes? *This* man didn't look like the monster she had made him out to be.

Had she been over-hasty in her condemnation of him? Wasn't it true that as soon as she had discovered who he was she had judged him through eyes coloured by the past, by her own hurt pride and foolish, adolescent spite? Simply by being here, he revived memories she would rather not remember, making her think of how stupidly and selfishly she had behaved, and those feelings had prejudiced her normally open mind.

Daniel seemed oblivious to her presence, lost in some private world of his own, his keen hazel eyes scanning the countryside, and for the moment she was content to have it that way, content to watch and absorb the powerful attraction of the strongly carved face and let time hang suspended for a moment. She felt as if she were poised on the brink of a new beginning and, like a child who took time to remove the wrappings on a special present as carefully as possible in order to prolong the moment of pleasure as much as it could, she was happy to wait a while for that new beginning to come about.

'I used to come up here nearly every day in the summer,' Daniel's quiet voice came unexpectedly, making her start slightly. 'And this was my hiding-place whenever things got on top of me.'

Jessica was watching him with such intensity that she noticed the small reaction, the swift hardening of his face, the sudden compression of his lips as his eyes lighted on some particular spot in the distance. Following the direction of his gaze, she spotted the large, imposing house half hidden by trees down in the valley.

'Of course! I'd forgotten that your father lives here.'

And forgotten John's story of Daniel's relationship with his stepmother, a small voice added inside her head, making her falter uneasily. A foolish mistake that, and one that made a nonsense of her half-formed re-assessment of Daniel's character.

Daniel suddenly seemed to become aware of the fact that he was still holding her hand, and he released it so abruptly that it fell to her side with an uncomfortable, jarring movement.

'I haven't seen him for years,' he said, and Jessica's heart jumped nervously as she recalled his reaction to her comment about his father on the night at the theatre, the swift change in his expression that had stripped away all that potent, smiling charm. She searched his face apprehensively, looking for the tightness of muscle, the deepening of the fine lines around his nose and mouth that would indicate the return of that disturbing, frightening mood, and was relieved to see instead an abstracted, thoughtful expression, as if his mind were far away. 'I doubt if he knows I'm around.'

'But surely he's been to the show? When I opened the Jester, all my family came along to celebrate——'

She knew the words were a mistake as soon as she uttered them. The party to celebrate the opening of the restaurant had been a wonderfully happy occasion, with her parents and three brothers there to share in her pride at her new venture. Even Martin, her youngest brother, who lived in jeans and sweatshirts, had decked himself out in a suit and tie for the occasion.

But she had never hurt her parents as Daniel must have devastated his father. What sort of man could have behaved in that appalling way?

'My father wouldn't have time for that.' Daniel's tone was harsh. 'He's far too busy with the fourth Mrs Tyson.'

'The *fourth*!'

Jessica couldn't stop herself, the exclamation slipped out before she had time to think, and she took an instinctive step backwards, fearful that she might have provoked the dark anger she had seen in his face in the theatre bar.

Daniel nodded, his wide mouth set in a grim line.

'At least my new stepmother is more his age.' He swung round suddenly so that she saw the bitter cynicism that darkened his eyes. 'He married the previous one on her twenty-fifth birthday.'

Jessica hunted for something to say that would not spark off the explosion she felt was simmering just below the surface. Was this some sort of test? Was he trying to find out if she had heard the story about his affair with his father's young wife? Fear made her cautious. She could not be unaware of the fact that she was alone with Daniel on this deserted hillside; she had no wish to risk the possible repercussions if that savage temper was unleashed.

'Few people worry about age differences in marriage these days,' she said carefully. 'Sometimes things can work out very well——'

She flinched away from the sound of his laughter which, harsh and bitter, without a trace of humour in it, shattered the still quiet of the hillside.

'*Sometimes* they do,' he agreed sardonically, 'but——'

He broke off abruptly, but the contempt that had thickened his voice struck home to Jessica, sending shock-waves reverberating through her body. Only a few minutes before, she had come very close to liking Daniel. She had been prepared to completely rethink her attitude, to judge him without the shadows the past left on the present obscuring the issue, but now she found herself mentally taking several hasty steps away from him again.

How could a son behave like this towards his father? By his own admission, he hadn't seen Melvyn Tyson for years, a fact which seemed to confirm John's story. A strongly family-orientated person herself, Jessica visited her own parents at least once a week, and she knew how much they looked forward to her visits. It would devastate them if she never came near them, particularly if, like Daniel, she had been an only child.

'Come on.' Daniel's voice broke into her thoughts. 'It's time we had lunch. I thought we'd go to the Traveller's Rest.'

Jessica tried hard to maintain some sort of conversation on the way back to the car, wanting to stick to her original plan of distracting his interest from Miriam, but her heart wasn't in it. The relaxed mood of the morning had been shattered, and she found it hard to think of anything to say. Daniel's curt, monosyllabic answers were positively discouraging, so in the end she gave up and retreated into her own thoughts, which were every bit as uncomfortable as her attempts to talk had been.

The overwhelming feeling that assailed her was one of terrible disappointment: disappointment for the loss of the ease they had shared earlier, for the destruction of her fragile, barely formed hopes of a new beginning, and for the way Daniel had proved himself to be the heartless man she had believed him to be. That harshly cynical laugh had revealed his character far more clearly than any words could ever do.

Jessica shivered as she heard the sound of that laugh once more inside her head. If Daniel could be so unfeeling towards his father, then what chance was there of convincing him that he would hurt Miriam terribly if he continued to flirt with her as he had been doing? He had shown no sign of respecting or even caring about the fact that she was married, and if his father had been married four times that was hardly an example of long-standing commitment.

Like father, like son. The phrase came into her mind with a disturbing force as her eyes went to the silent, withdrawn man at her side, seeing how his face had become a distant, cold mask, those heavy lids hooding his eyes, hiding what he was thinking. She had been wrong to think she had seen him clearly before. Now her eyes were really open and she saw that his was a hard, unyielding face, looking as if it had been carved out of granite, with nothing soft or gentle about it. And this man threatened Miriam's happiness. Well, he wasn't going to mess up her friend's life as he had his father's, not if she had anything to do with it!

* * *

'What do you think of the food? Your professional opinion, that is.'

Jessica had become so accustomed to Daniel's silent state that his words made her start in surprise. Even on their arrival at the pub he had kept conversation to a minimum, simply asking what she wanted to eat and drink, but now he appeared to have thrown off his dark mood.

'It's fine.' Her gesture indicated the bowl of thick, home-made vegetable soup and the ploughman's lunch she had ordered. 'Simple but sustaining, just the sort of thing you need after a trek across the moors. This soup is every bit as good as anything we offer at the Jester.'

'That was something that surprised me. When I came to the restaurant I expected that the menu would be much more exotic. After some of the meals, I've had down south, I have to admit that it came as a very pleasant change.'

The wry twist to his mouth, the gleam of humour in his eyes, had Jessica smiling involuntarily in response.

'Can you imagine any Yorkshireman being satisfied with *nouvelle cuisine*? I try to stick to the best of English cooking with everything as fresh as possible and all prepared on the premises. I decided that that was the best policy when I was planning the restaurant, and it seems to have worked—we're doing a roaring trade.'

'You don't cook the meals yourself, though?'

'No. I did at the beginning, but when the Jester became so popular I had to make a choice between running it properly and being the chef. There was too much involved in doing both—I wasn't getting any time to myself.'

'But you miss it?'

Jessica was surprised that Daniel had caught the note of regret in her voice; she had thought it was faint enough not to be noticed.

'Yes, I do. I really enjoyed that part of it. Some nights were totally mad—— At the beginning there was just Miriam and myself to do everything—cooking, serving at the tables—and we were rushed off our feet, but I loved every minute of it. I had something that was all mine, and it was a real challenge trying to make a go of it.'

She paused, her smile reflective as she recalled those early days.

'I'm making a lot more money now the restaurant's established and a success, but I miss those crazy times. They were nerve-racking, too—everything depended on me. I'd talked about owning my own restaurant for years and now it was actually happening—it was make or break time. I had my dream, but I had to prove I could make it work.'

Daniel nodded slowly.

'So many people drift through life, opting for safety and security, never taking any risks, but never knowing the satisfaction that comes from doing what you really want. Sometimes striking out on your own can be like setting out to climb some huge mountain—it's terrifying, but exhilarating too. You might fall flat on your face—lose everything—or you might get to the top, but you'll never know until you *try*. And when you know what you really want to do in life, you have to go for it, take that chance, otherwise you might just as well stop living.'

Looking deep into Daniel's eyes, Jessica was surprised to detect a depth of understanding and empathy with her own feelings that gave her an unexpected insight into his own life.

'Is that why you did what you did? After all, you have——'

'Changed horses in mid-stream?' Daniel supplied for her when she hesitated, unsure of the right words. 'I suppose to someone who knew me at college it must look as if that's what I've done.'

'Well, everyone thought you were destined for some sort of high-flying legal career. No one would have expected you'd become——'

'A crude, arrogant, tasteless bore who just happens to think he's funny?'

Though sardonic, the beautiful voice had none of the aggressive, attacking quality she had come to fear, but, all the same, hot colour flooded into Jessica's cheeks.

'No—look, I'm sorry! I take that back quite unreservedly. I didn't mean it—not personally. John—the man I was with—wanted me to go to the show with him, and I was trying to find a way out of it, so I said the first thing that came into my mind. It wasn't meant about you—though I have to admit that until now I've never really been impressed by any comedian. But I really enjoyed your show—in fact I loved it—honestly!'

The silence that followed her outburst was unnerving. Daniel leaned back in his chair, his eyes, deep green in the afternoon sunshine, surveying her face with a slow, intent scrutiny that had her biting her lip in apprehension. Which man would respond to what she had said? The Daniel she had glimpsed briefly in their earlier, companionable mood that morning, or the hard, cynically amoral man who had treated his father so appallingly?

'Thank you,' he said at last, his voice low and slightly husky; only then did Jessica become aware of the fact that she had been holding her breath, and she let it escape in a long sigh of relief, his quiet response giving her the courage to venture another question.

'So why did you end up on the stage? You showed no sign of any interest in it at school, and, if you don't mind my saying so, you're a very serious sort of person for a comic.'

That had his wide mouth curling into a smile.

'Don't they say that every clown really wants to play Hamlet?' he said lightly, the smile warming his eyes in a way that made her breath catch in her throat. 'No— when I was younger I was determined that anything to do with showbusiness or acting was the last thing I would ever do.'

Suddenly there was a worrying edge to his voice, and Jessica shifted uneasily in her seat at the thought of his earlier hostility towards his father. Her question had led her on to dangerous ground.

'I went to university to study law and I was convinced that I was going to make a career out of that. I walked straight into a really good job, one that should have set me up for life, and I was also very involved in local politics—there was even talk of my being put forward as a candidate for that constituency when the present MP retired, so I suppose in most people's eyes I had it made. But then I found that my ideas had changed.'

Daniel paused, pushing one hand through the thick brightness of his hair, his eyes slightly unfocused, as if he was looking back at the past, at his younger self.

'I got involved with the stage by accident. At university, a girl I was dating was producing a play and one of the actors had to drop out just a week before they were due to open.'

A grin surfaced briefly, its boyish appeal tugging at Jessica's heart. That beautiful voice had worked its magic again, and she sat entranced, oblivious to the chatter and noise around her, intent on his story, wanting to know what had brought about such a major change in the life of this man who had had everything anyone could ask for in the way of professional success, and yet had thrown it all up for a precarious and uncertain existence.

'He broke his leg on the football pitch and could hardly play the romantic lead in plaster and on crutches. Nancy was desperate; she didn't know which way to turn. Even if she could find someone to take his place, could they learn the part—and it was a *big* part—in the little time they had left?'

Another smile, softer this time, curved his lips, and Jessica was stunned by the effect it had on her as she realised that the sudden, stabbing sensation deep inside her was caused by a flash of envy of the unknown Nancy.

'Anyway, someone suggested that I could do the part. I knew as much about it as the original actor—I was *very* involved with Nan——'

Jessica winced mentally at a second stabbing pain.

'So much so that I'd overcome my prejudice against acting and actors, and I'd been to every rehearsal with her. I knew the whole play backwards. So I tried, and it worked—but by the end of the first rehearsal I was hooked. It was as if I'd found a part of my life that had always been missing up till then—the final piece that made my personal jigsaw complete. Once the bug had got me, it wouldn't let go. I acted in several student productions and found to my amazement that I had a particular gift for comedy. But it wasn't what I wanted

to do for a living. I wanted a job that had meaning—
that would make a positive contribution to society. I'd
seen such injustice, prejudice and plain, blind stupidity
around me, and I wanted to fight that.'

'But you did that in your show. You made people
laugh, but you also made them think—you certainly
made *me* think. Making people laugh at their own
prejudices must be one of the best ways of making them
realise just how stupid they are.'

'That's exactly the point.'

The warm, appreciative look Daniel turned on her was
like an arrow winging its way straight to her heart, devastating in its impact, obliterating her dislike, her doubts
and fears about him, and leaving her dangerously vulnerable to the hypnotic appeal of that glorious voice.

'That's what I try to do now, but it took me a while
to see things that way. It happened when I was involved
in a campaign to prevent the council closing a children's
home. Those kids had been together for years—they were
like a family, and if it was closed they'd be split up, sent
to different places all around the county, but the council
said the place was uneconomical. There was a public
meeting and it degenerated into a real slanging match,
everyone too busy trading insults to think about the real
point of issue. I got so disgusted, I just stood up and
started to speak——'

Daniel's hands spread in a gesture of resignation.

'I made them laugh. They calmed down and started
to think clearly, and eventually worked out a com-
promise that satisfied everyone. That was when I realised that humour isn't just for relaxation—that, used
properly, it can be more effective than any rhetoric in
getting a message across. I've tried to use it that way
ever since. I want my act to reflect people's concerns

about the issues of the day, and I hope it works like that.'

He had stopped speaking for a few moments before Jessica came back to herself. She had been so absorbed in his story that she had ignored her half-eaten meal, too caught up in what he was saying to think of swallowing a single mouthful.

'I'm glad you told me,' she said at last, her voice slightly shaken because, as she'd looked into those clear hazel eyes, she had experienced another shock like the one that had assailed her on the moors overlooking his father's house.

She had dismissed Daniel as a shallow, arrogant, selfish womaniser, a man who had gone into show-business to boost his own ego, but clearly there was more to him than that. The story he had told her had come from the heart, revealing a thoughtful, caring man, one she felt she could easily come to admire very much.

'I'm glad I told you too. I——'

The sound of the pub door opening interrupted what he had been about to say, drawing his eyes from Jessica's face to the couple who had just come in. Immediately his head went back, his eyes darkening, the tension that emanated from every tightly held muscle so strongly evident of some hostility that instinctively Jessica swung round in her seat to see who or what had changed his mood so dramatically.

From the moment her gaze fell on the man at the bar she knew exactly who he was. There was only one person he *could* be, and that was Daniel's father. Tall, dark, heavily built, Melvyn Tyson was a big man in every way. He had some extra inches in height on his son and the weight he had gained since she had last seen him on television made him look like a wrestler in contrast to Daniel's compact strength.

Already alerted by Daniel's reaction, Jessica felt her muscles clench tight in apprehension as she saw the way his face had changed, his skin losing colour where it seemed stretched tight over his cheekbones, his eyes watching every move his father made so that inevitably, after a few minutes, the other man sensed his scrutiny and turned his head in their direction.

In the split second in which the two men's eyes locked together Jessica saw shock, recognition and a mixture of joy and something echoing her own unease cross the older man's face before he shouldered his way across the room towards them.

'Daniel!'

It was his son's voice, the rich tones roughened by raw emotion. Beside her, Daniel had got to his feet.

'Father.'

The single word was curt, clipped, painfully, formally polite, and he pointedly ignored the hand that Melvyn Tyson half raised towards him, then let drop to his side. There was a distinct pause then Daniel's eyes moved from his father's face to a point behind his shoulder, and he inclined his head slightly in a greeting so coldly distant it was more like an insult.

'Mrs Tyson.'

Only then did Jessica become aware of the small figure standing like a silent shadow at Melvyn Tyson's side. The new Mrs Tyson was not at all what she had expected. From Daniel's scathing comments, she had imagined a bright, young, stylish creature, the sort of pretty girl older men were traditionally believed to fall for, not this plump, almost matronly person with neat dark hair curling softly about a round, clear-complexioned face

in which a pair of wide blue eyes were her best feature.
The stepmother Daniel had known might have been very
young, but this woman was much nearer her husband's
age.

'There's no need for formality, my name is Kaye,' she
said, her voice calm, revealing no hint of having noticed
the deliberate coldness with which Daniel had greeted
her. 'I'm glad to meet you at last, Daniel. It was a pity
you couldn't come to our wedding.'

The reproof was so mild that it would have been easy
to miss it, but, watching Daniel's face, Jessica knew it
had struck home as for a moment he looked nonplussed, almost shame-faced. But he recovered almost
immediately.

'I'm afraid I was busy. I had bookings that had been
made months before which I had to keep to.'

Small though she was, Kaye Tyson was clearly in no
way intimidated by Daniel's physical strength and,
equally evidently, neither was she deceived by the offhand
way in which he offered the explanation.

'Of course.' There was just the tiniest bit of bite in
the soft tones. 'Your career's really beginning to take
off, isn't it? And I'm not surprised. We saw the
show——'

That threw him. Startled hazel eyes looked straight
into calm blue ones, and what he saw there brought a
sudden rush of colour to his cheeks. Alerted by a small
movement, Jessica saw the way the restless tapping of
one hand against his thigh revealed his unease far more
eloquently than words. He and his father were like two
wary terriers circling each other nervously, each one
waiting for the other to attack.

'Look, why don't you sit down?' she put in hastily,
pulling out a chair. 'Kaye——?'

There was a flash of gratitude in the look the other woman turned on her, and intuitively she knew she had an ally in Kaye Tyson. Beside his wife, Melvyn Tyson too lowered himself into a chair.

'Daniel——' Jessica prompted when he stubbornly remained standing.

'We don't have time—I have to be going——'

His face was granite-hard, his hostility so tangible she could feel it like sparks of electricity on the air, but she refused to let that shake her.

'Where to? The theatre? You told me yourself you don't have to be there until six.' There was a strong satisfaction in pulling that particular rug from under his feet. It was time Daniel faced up to the past, and it looked as if this was about the only chance he was ever likely to get; clearly he had avoided his father like the plague since the time he had left Scarby. 'Besides, I haven't finished my lunch—so sit down.'

What she would do if he refused, if he simply turned and walked out, she didn't know. He was perfectly capable of doing just that, she suspected, and knew a rush of relief when, unexpectedly, without further argument, Daniel subsided into his chair at her side. Not daring to push him any further, Jessica turned to Melvyn Tyson.

'I'd better introduce myself—I'm Jessica Terry.'

Brown eyes, several shades darker than his son's, met hers, lighting with the famous smile which almost, but not completely erased the shadows from his face.

'I've heard of you—you're known as the Jester's Girl.'

'That's right. Have you ever been in the restaurant?'

'No.' It was Kaye who spoke. 'We've been living very quietly lately. Mel——'

A swift glance at her husband sought approval for what she was about to say.

'My husband has been rather ill. The doctors say he should rest.'

Hypersensitive to the man sitting darkly silent at her side, Jessica caught the almost imperceptible hiss of his breath between his teeth that revealed that he wasn't as immune to feeling as he would like to pretend. So why didn't he show that? What held him back? Pride? Damn his stubbornness! He had the perfect opportunity to breach the gulf that had grown up between himself and his father, so why didn't he take it?

'But you went to see Daniel's show.'

The tiny hairs on the back of Jessica's neck lifted in instinctive reaction as she felt the waves of hostility emanating from Daniel at the way she had brought the conversation round to him, their force so palpable that it dried her mouth, making her voice unsteady as she continued.

'Did you enjoy it?'

'I did, very much.' Genuine admiration rang in Melvyn's voice, and his eyes went to his son, the longing in them tearing at Jessica's heart. 'It was the first chance I've had to get to see what you do, and I must say I was impressed. I didn't realise——'

He broke off abruptly as Daniel's glass, which he had lifted to his lips, was slammed back down on to the table with a loud crash.

'There's no need for this,' he declared bitingly. 'I'd prefer it if you'd drop the concerned father act—it's fooling no one.'

'Daniel!'

'But——'

'That's not true——'

Three voices, Jessica's, Melvyn's and Kaye's, clashed in the same second and then fell silent again as Daniel pushed back his chair violently and got to his feet.

'And now, if you'll excuse me, I'm afraid I really have to go,' he announced with an icy formality that seemed almost nightmarishly unreal after his outburst of a moment before. 'I'll wait for you in the car, Jessica. But I'll be leaving in five minutes.' He glanced pointedly at his watch. 'With you or without you.'

And, without another glance in his father's direction, he turned on his heel and strode towards the door.

'I'm sorry,' Jessica said unevenly, to fill the silence that followed his departure.

Melvyn Tyson's smile was slow and resigned.

'Please don't upset yourself, Miss Terry. I appreciate what you were trying to do, but my relationship with my son has always been a difficult one. We're too much alike—both plagued with an excess of stubborn pride. He was brought up by his mother when our marriage broke up, and so, naturally, his loyalty has always been given to her. I'm afraid I was too involved with my career and I made a lot of mistakes—the worst one being my neglect of Daniel when he was young. We completely lost touch until he was nineteen. That was when I bought a house here and six months later he came to live with me for a while. It—didn't work out.'

He paused, taking a deep swallow from his drink, and Kaye's hand went out to cover her husband's, giving it a quick, warm squeeze. Jessica felt desperately uncomfortable, knowing he was completely unaware of the fact that she knew exactly what he was talking about, that she had heard the whole sorry story which, even now, his love for his son made him want to keep hidden.

Oh, *damn* Daniel Tyson! How could he hurt his father like this?

'Daniel's mother had just died and his emotions were still very raw. He believed I'd abandoned them both—she'd been very ill and there had been very little money. But I didn't know——'

'Mel——' Kaye put in as he broke off, shaking his head in distress. 'Don't upset yourself.'

Her clear eyes went to Jessica's face.

'Daniel hurt my husband very badly, Miss Terry. He walked out of the house, swore he'd never come back, and he's kept to that vow. Apart from seeing him on stage, this is the first time they've met in nine years.'

Jessica knew her feelings must show on her face. What sort of man could behave in this way? Her thoughts went to her own parents, to the two days she had spent in their company only the previous weekend. How could she exist, knowing they were still alive, living in the same country, and yet never, ever seeing them?

'How well do you know my son, Miss Terry? What are your feelings for him?'

'I——' Melvyn Tyson's question disconcerted Jessica. It wasn't one she found easy to answer. 'I don't really know him at all. We were at college together for a year, but I only really met up with him again this week——'

And how did she *feel* about him? She didn't know. It seemed as if, in the few days since she had met Daniel again, she had experienced almost every emotion a human being was capable of feeling. Anger, disgust, contempt and abhorrence for the way he had treated his father, together with a dislike bordering on hatred, those were the negative things; but there was a positive side too—admiration, respect for the way his mind worked, the laughter his act had provoked. She had felt an empathy with him—and of course there was the passion he awoke in her, a disconcerting honesty forced her to admit. The most intense emotion she had felt had been that overpoweringly powerful rush of desire that had swamped her when he'd kissed her. But what all those feelings added up to, she couldn't even begin to express.

'But he seems to listen to you——'

Jessica was about to deny that statement vehemently when she remembered how, at her urging, Daniel had sat down when he had been quite adamant that he was leaving. He had only stayed for a few minutes, it was true, but he *had* done as she asked.

Melvyn Tyson was leaning forward now, his brown eyes dark and intent.

'Daniel and I fought over something I'd rather forget. I'm at an age when my contemporaries are looking forward to seeing their grandchildren, and I'd like to hope that perhaps, one day, I could hold Daniel's child. I've made mistakes, I'm only too willing to admit that, but I'd give the world to put those mistakes right, build a new relationship. Talk to my son, Miss Terry. Tell him all I want is to put the past behind us and start again.'

It was impossible to resist the appeal in those eyes, the emotion in the voice that was so like his son's. Jessica didn't know if she could possibly have any influence with Daniel; she only knew she had to try.

But would he even listen? The man who had stalked out of the bar minutes before was hardly likely to give her a chance to speak, but the other Daniel—the man she had been talking to before his father arrived, the man who cared about prejudice and injustice and used his intelligence, his brilliant wit against them, *he* would care, would want to put things right. Perhaps there had been some terrible mistake, one that Daniel could explain, if she could just get past that appalling stubborn pride.

'I'll try, Mr Tyson. I don't know if it'll do any good but——'

She broke off abruptly as a sudden thought struck her, the recollection of Daniel's intractable, 'I'll be leaving in five minutes,' bringing her to her feet in a rush. If she was to have any chance of talking to him, she had to do it now, before he left, as she had no doubt he would do if she was one second later than the time he had stipulated. If she let him go now, the mood he was in, there was little chance that she would see him again before his final show was over and he was on his way to Doncaster.

'I have to go—he won't wait——'

In her anxiety she couldn't form the words coherently, but there was no need to explain. Both Melvyn and Kaye had heard Daniel's ultimatum and understood the reason for her urgency.

'Give him my love——' Melvyn Tyson's words barely reached her ears as she hurried away, breaking into a run as soon as she was out of the bar.

Her heart beating high up in her throat, Jessica dashed round to the car park, skidding to a halt as she saw that Daniel's car still stood where he had left it when they had arrived. The sight of the dark figure in the driving seat, powerful shoulders hunched, hands clenched on the wheel, did nothing to ease the racing of her pulse, and her legs felt unsteady beneath her as she approached the car and met the hard force of his stony-eyed gaze as he turned his head to face her through the open passenger door.

'I was just about to go.'

As an opening it wasn't in the least encouraging, and every careful phrase that had flashed through her mind in her mad dash from the bar flew from her thoughts so that she rushed into unthinking, unprepared speech. 'Why did you walk out like that? Your father wanted to talk to you!'

Those fierce tiger's eyes met hers unblinkingly, no trace of warmth lighting them.

'My father and I have nothing to say to each other. We might as well be two complete strangers who just happen to share the same surname.'

'That isn't true! He cares about you! He's a sad man, Daniel—a lonely man——'

'He has his wife.' The words slashed through the air like a razor-sharp knife.

'Yes, he has Kaye—and she's not what you think. She cares for him, loves him—anyone who isn't half blind can see that. But you're his son—his own flesh and blood!'

'You sound like some trashy novel.' Daniel's tone was scathing. 'I should have known you'd fall for his grieving father routine. Women never could resist my father— and he could never resist them!'

Once more that harsh, humourless laugh made Jessica quail inside.

'What did he tell you, Mystery? Did he say *why* I walked out of his house—why I haven't seen him for nine years?'

There was a new and disturbing intensity about his voice, something that sharpened that changeable gaze until Jessica felt it might burn through skin and bone like a laser beam, penetrating right to her heart.

'He said that your loyalties were with your mother.' She couldn't tell him she knew the whole truth, es-

pecially not when his father had been so careful to keep
it from her. 'And that you believed he'd treated her
badly.'

'Which he did. He abandoned her for the first pretty
little starlet who threw herself at him, and never thought
twice about her again. While he was making a fortune
as the housewives' heart-throb, she was struggling to
bring me up on the pittance he sent her. He didn't even
know she was ill until the week before she died. Did he
tell you that?'

'He said he'd made mistakes and he was sorry for
them. But you hurt him too. He tried to be a father to
you; rather late, perhaps, but he tried—and you just
walked out——'

'Just walked out?' Daniel's voice burned acrid with
bitterness as he echoed her words. 'I knew he wouldn't
admit the truth. I didn't *walk* anywhere, Mystery. I was
thrown out. Don't you want to know why?'

It was too late to hold back now. 'I know why—but
I didn't believe it.'

'Well, believe it!' Daniel declared hardily. 'And then
see if you're still determined to arrange this reconciliation that's suddenly so very important to you, because
it happens to be true. My father threw me out of his
house because he found me in bed with his wife—the
Mrs Tyson of the time—the third, I believe she was.'

For a second Jessica's mind went blank with shock,
her eyes wide grey pools of distress above colourless
cheeks. She felt as if something very precious to her had
just died, the image of Daniel as a caring, admirable
human being shrivelling to dust before her eyes. There
had been no trace of feeling or remorse in his cold, hard
declaration. A terrible sense of loss and desolation swept

through her, explosively combined with wild, furious anger.

'You *animal*!' The memory of her own foolish hope that there might be some possible explanation for what had happened, and disgust at her own naïveté, fuelled her fury, obliterating all thought of what Melvyn Tyson had asked her to say. 'You lousy, stinking sewer rat! What sort of son would do that to his father? You disgust me! You're the most hateful man I've ever met!'

Reaching out, she caught hold of the car door and slammed it shut with as much force as she could manage, using the violent movement to express her churning feelings.

'Get out of my life, Daniel Tyson!' she yelled, not caring who heard. 'Get out and stay out! I knew you were trouble from the moment I saw you, but I didn't know how much. Now I do—and I never—*ever*—want to see you again!'

Through a red haze of anger she saw Daniel lift a hand as if he would have opened the door again, but then he let it drop back on to the wheel. A moment later the car's engine roared into life and Jessica had to step back hastily as the tyres screeched over the gravel, heading for the road at an insanely dangerous speed.

CHAPTER SIX

'JESS, I've had a wonderful idea!'

Deep in the end-of-month accounts, Jessica could only manage an inarticulate murmur that might have been an indication of interest in response to Miriam's excited announcement. She had been at her desk all morning, entangled in bills, costs and profits, the figures dancing before her eyes, refusing to add up and coming to a different total each time she tried, until she was ready to scream.

She had been in that frame of mind all weekend, grouchy, out of sorts and unable to concentrate, and the worst thing about it was that she knew exactly where it stemmed from. It had begun with the confrontation with Daniel in the pub car park.

After Daniel had driven away, she had started to walk, choosing a direction at random, not caring where she was going, only knowing that she could not go back and face Melvyn and Kaye now she knew the truth. How could she see Daniel's father's concern for his son, his longing to put the past behind him, and then tell him that the son he cared so much about wasn't worth the love he felt for him? Melvyn Tyson might be able to forgive and forget, but Daniel's reaction when he had told her about being found in bed with his stepmother had revealed no shame or remorse at what had happened. He had flung the declaration at her, hard-faced and arrogant as ever, his cold, unemotional statement seeming to defy her to make something of a revelation that he knew must shock and disgust any reasonable person. If Melvyn had seen his son's reaction, he would know that there was no hope of any reconciliation with his son and, personally, Jessica felt he was better off without that son who cared nothing for his father—but she couldn't bring herself to say so to his face.

'Jessica, you're not listening!' Miriam's complaint brought her out of her uncomfortable memories, and she shook her head slightly to try to clear it of the clinging fog of gloom that had clouded it ever since Friday.

'Sorry! It's these damn accounts. I can't make head or tail of them.'

Which was not a problem that she usually had. She had always seen the financial side of her business as a challenge; balancing expenses with profits, planning budgets, was part of the job and she prided herself on tackling it with a clear mind, keeping careful, accurate records that delighted her accountant. But today that frame of mind had deserted her. With a sigh she put down her pen.

'So what's the great idea, then?'

'It's about Dan—Daniel Tyson.'

At the sound of that name Jessica's heart seemed to stop, then jolt back into action in a sickeningly uneven way, an uncomfortable, queasy sensation settling in her stomach. In the disturbed state of mind that had plagued her since Friday, her dread of a phone call from Melvyn to ask if she had talked to Daniel, and the general bustle of a weekend in the restaurant, she had forgotten her fears for Miriam, but now they came rushing back with increased force as she considered the implications of what had happened with regard to her friend.

She had woken this morning with a sense of relief at the thought that at least Daniel had left Scarby, but, caught up in her own concerns, she had forgotten that he had still been in town on Saturday—when Miriam had been on her weekend off. Had anything happened between them?

'What about—him?' She couldn't say Daniel's name, feeling it might choke her if she tried.

'I was talking to Emma Hardy—you remember her, she works at the Civic Theatre. She was telling me how every one of Dan's shows had been sold out and people were still clamouring for seats. She said they could have sold every ticket two or three times over—Jess, are you listening?'

'Yes.' With an effort Jessica composed her face into what she hoped was an interested expression, though it was far harder to keep her thoughts under control. She couldn't be unaware of the warmth of that 'Dan', the affectionate shortening of his name that even his father hadn't been able to use. 'Go on.'

'Well, you know you asked me to come up with some ideas for publicity—new ways to attract people to the restaurant? I've been thinking about it lately, and I know I've found just the thing. Dan says he does cabaret as well as shows and——'

'*When* did he say that?' Jessica couldn't help herself. The thought of Miriam on her own at the weekend—when Daniel Tyson was still around—had pushed her into the unconsidered question.

'Over lunch.' Miriam was clearly disconcerted by the sharpness of her friend's tone. 'You remember—on Thursday.'

'Oh, yes.' Jessica could not meet Miriam's eyes, afraid that her relief might show in her own.

'Anyway, Emma said that they've had loads of enquiries about the possibility of him coming back, doing another set of shows, but they didn't have any plans for that yet. You know we've often discussed the idea of holding a cabaret some evenings, and when Dan's finished this tour he has a couple of weeks free, so I thought——'

'No!' Jessica had finally caught the drift of what Miriam was saying. 'Definitely not.'

'*Why* not?' Miriam looked nonplussed, confused by Jessica's vehemence. 'Dan's really popular, Jess. Everyone I've talked to raves about him. We'd be packed out if he appeared here. And I've already planned some publicity,' she added plaintively. 'After all, we are called the *Jester*——'

'I don't think it would work.'

The lie burned on Jessica's tongue. It was a good idea—a brilliant idea—and under any other circumstances she would have jumped at it. But she *couldn't* do business with Daniel Tyson to save her life, couldn't be responsible for bringing him back to Scarby. Aside from her own feelings, it would hurt his father too much, and what about Miriam? How could she ever forgive herself if she was the cause of her friend's continuing her dangerous friendship with Daniel?

'How's Al?' she asked, in what she hoped was an offhand way in a clumsy attempt to change the subject.

Miriam blinked hard in surprise, then a look of annoyance crossed her face.

'Jess, I just don't believe what I'm hearing! You wanted some publicity ideas, I've come up with a cracker—and all you can say is, "How's Al?"'

'He *is* your husband,' Jessica said pointedly. 'Did he have to work this weekend?'

She regretted the question as soon as she saw the change in Miriam's face, the pale, peaky look that her excitement about her plans for a cabaret had driven away returning so that she looked drawn and unhappy.

'No, he didn't *have* to. The overtime was optional, but he took it just the same.'

'On your weekend off!'

What was happening to these two? In the past they had appeared inseparable, now their marriage seemed to be falling apart.

'Saturday *and* Sunday,' Miriam confirmed flatly. 'If Dan hadn't called round I'd have been on my——'

'*Daniel* called round?' Jessica couldn't keep the shock from her voice. 'You saw Daniel Tyson this weekend?'

'He came for lunch on Saturday in return for taking me out last Thursday.' Miriam's tone was worryingly defiant. 'And he called in on Sunday, too—to say goodbye.'

If she could believe that was true, she would feel so much happier about things. If Daniel had gone for good, then perhaps Miriam would get back to normal, concentrate on repairing her marriage without the dangerous distraction of Daniel Tyson's attentions.

'What have you got against Dan, Jess?' Miriam's question came unexpectedly, leaving Jessica at a loss for words. 'You can't still be angry about the way he snubbed you, not after nine years!'

Why did she have to bring that up now? Jessica didn't want to remember the past, didn't want to be reminded of the way she had thrown herself at Daniel, using all the immature wiles of which she was capable. A hot flush of embarrassment suffused her body. Oh, she had thought herself irresistible, fluttering her eyelashes and speaking in a low, husky and, she had believed, sexually enticing voice. Christmas was approaching and, among the girls at the college at least, it seemed that there was only one topic of conversation—the question of whom Daniel Tyson would take to the Christmas disco.

Jessica had had several invitations already, she had no shortage of possible escorts, but she hadn't accepted any of them definitely. Daniel Tyson had intrigued her from the moment he had arrived, his apparent lack of interest in girls a challenge she was unable to resist. She had determined that *she* would be his partner, no matter what she had to do to achieve it.

When ten days of subtle hints and careful flirting showed no sign of bringing results, and with the disco only a week away, Jessica had resolved on more positive action. Planning her move carefully, she had made discreet enquiries and had discovered that on most afternoons Daniel stayed at college late, working in the library. So the next day she had joined him there, sitting at another table and making a pretence of studying, though it was impossible to concentrate. Her gaze kept drifting to where Daniel sat in the far corner, his head bent over his books, his pen moving rapidly over the page. She might not have been in the room for all the notice he gave her, and his total indifference firmed her resolve, stiffening her pride, so that when it was announced that the library was closing she bundled her books into her bag far more quickly than Daniel, who performed the same task with obvious reluctance; she was just behind him as he reached the door.

'Mind if I walk along with you?' she asked with what she hoped was an air of casual insouciance, knowing that the stop at which he caught his bus was in the direction of her own home.

'If you like.'

His response was hardly encouraging, but Jessica didn't care. She was alone with him at last, they had

been the only two people in the library, and she was sure
she could use the time available to her profitably.

She tried a couple of remarks about work, the
Christmas play, but, getting only monosyllabic answers,
decided to cut out any attempt at chat and get straight
to the point.

'Are you looking forward to the disco? From all accounts, it's going to be a lot of fun.'

'I hadn't planned on going.'

'Oh, but you must! Everyone's going!' The realisation that the fact that he hadn't planned on going meant
that he couldn't already have asked anyone to go with
him had her rushing on impetuously, 'Don't you have
a partner, is that it? Well, as a matter of fact, neither
do I.'

Daniel came to a halt so suddenly that she had walked
several feet past him before she realised, and she turned
to find him standing, feet planted widely apart, hands
on his narrow hips, surveying her through narrowed eyes.

'Just what is all this about, Jessica?' he asked, a hard
note roughening his voice.

'It's not about anything!' Painfully aware of the fact
that she sounded shrill and nervous, Jessica hastily ad-
justed her voice to the low, sensual tone she felt would
be more appealing. 'It's just that if you needed someone
to go with, I thought——'

She broke off awkwardly, her confidence threatened
by the way his mouth had twisted.

'You thought?' Daniel prompted, leaning back against
the wall and folding his arms across his chest, his eyes
sweeping over her in lazy appraisal. 'Go on, Jessica, tell
me what you thought.'

'I thought we might go together.' Encouraged by the
way his lips curved into a smile, she plunged on, 'I've

no one to go with either, and it's a pity to miss out on one of the social events of the year.'

Too late she saw that the smile was not one of encouragement and appreciation, but of satisfaction that his assumption about what she was going to say had been correct. Only now did she see the cynical light in his eyes, sending a sensation like cold pins and needles creeping over her skin.

'Thanks for the invitation, but no, thanks,' he drawled indolently. 'If I wanted a partner, I'm more than capable of finding my own.'

The jarring note in his voice made Jessica think that perhaps she hadn't phrased things as well as she might. It was possible that Daniel could have interpreted her invitation as a clumsy act of charity, a condescending offer from one of the in-crowd of college society to a newly arrived outsider.

'I don't think you understand! I've had plenty of offers of partners for the disco, but I'm not interested in any of them. *You're* the one I want to go with. The others mean nothing to me.'

'Jessica——'

Daniel unfolded his arms to push one hand through his hair, and Jessica interpreted the gesture as one of concession, her heart leaping at the thought that at last she was getting somewhere. The movement had removed the barrier of his arms across his chest, and recklessly she pressed home her advantage, moving close to nestle against him, winding her arms around his slim waist and letting her head rest on his shoulder.

'You're the one I want, Daniel. I don't care about anyone else.'

Under her cheek she felt the sudden jolt of his heart and the way his breathing changed, becoming rapid and uneven, and a thrill of triumph shot through her at the thought that the façade of indifference he had kept up for so long was finally beginning to crumble. Her own heart racing in excitement, she let her hands wander over his chest and, emboldened by the way he made no move to stop her, snuggled closer, tugging his tie loose at his neck and unbuttoning the collar of his shirt, pressing her lips to the warm skin she had exposed.

'Take me to the disco, Daniel. We'll have a wonderful time,' she murmured huskily. 'I promise you, you won't regret it.'

There was a moment of total, inexplicable silence, during which she felt Daniel's whole body tense like that of a wild animal poised for flight, but then suddenly, with a swiftness and strength that took her breath away, his arms closed round her and his lips came down hard on hers.

For a split second Jessica knew a sense of panic. This kiss, fierce and demanding, was not the sort of thing she had ever experienced before. It had an edge of danger, of threat to it that shook her sense of reality, making her feel as if the world had suddenly tilted sharply, throwing her precariously off balance. But then Daniel's lips softened against hers, becoming sensually beguiling, teasing her mouth open to deepen the kiss, and she followed his lead willingly, lifting her hands to lace them in the soft hair at the nape of his neck.

She barely felt the swift, efficient movements with which he dispensed with the buttons on her coat and the pink and white cardigan she wore underneath, so that the warmth of his hands through the thin cotton of her blouse came as an exquisite shock, making her catch her breath in delight. His touch was like a flame, warming her to a golden glow, flooding her veins with heat that even the breath of cold air on her skin couldn't cool as the final barrier of her blouse was eased away and those searching fingers closed around the white lacy cups that enclosed her breasts, teasingly caressing, his thumbs moving erotically over her responsive nipples.

She heard Daniel make a rough, harsh sound deep in his throat as his lips moved from her mouth and slid downward, etching a trail of fire along her throat and the sensitive flesh his hands had awakened. Her hands clenched convulsively in his hair, holding him close, wanting the moment and the delight it brought to last forever, but only seconds later he had lifted his head so that his cheek rested against hers.

'How far would you go, I wonder?' he whispered in her ear, so softly that for a few, bemused seconds she didn't take in the full impact of his words, hearing them as a huskily sensual enticement. 'How important is it to you, Jessie? How far will you go to get what you want?'

Then, before she had fully registered what her dazed mind had heard, he wrenched himself free from her restraining hands, pushing her away from him so that she fell against the wall, gasping with shock, her eyes wide and dark above colourless cheeks.

'You disgust me!' Daniel's voice was thick with loathing and contempt. 'Women! You're all the same! You use your bodies to get what you want because you think men are such blind, besotted fools that we'd do anything if you'd just let us touch you.'

'That isn't true!'

Sickeningly dizzy, and fighting waves of nausea that made her whole body shake, Jessica could barely get the words out, the shock of his violent rejection affecting her like a physical blow.

'Isn't it?' Daniel flung the words in her face. 'Look
at you!'

His savage gesture drew her attention to her gaping
coat and blouse, the flushed curves of her breasts above
the white lace and, below it, the all too obvious evidence
of the effect his caresses had had on her. With trembling
fingers Jessica pulled the edges of her blouse together
and held them, knowing she was incapable of the co-
ordination necessary to fasten the buttons.

'You didn't care where we were—who might have seen
us! You just saw a way to get what you wanted and used
it—used me—and all for——'

He broke off abruptly as if the words had choked him,
directing such a look of venomous loathing at her that
she shrank back against the wall.

'And all for a bloody date at the college disco!'

'*No!*' Jessica's voice rose to a shout. 'I *didn't*! I—
you——'

'So now it's *my* fault, is it?' Daniel's black cynicism
seared across her raw nerves. 'You didn't do anything.
I forced myself on you, tore your blouse open in spite
of your struggles—your protests. You didn't stand a
chance against my brutal lust—is that what you're trying
to claim?'

'No.' It was just a whisper, a miserable, thin thread
of sound. Much as she wished she could, she couldn't
claim that he had assaulted her. 'I didn't mean things
to go that far...'

Her voice failed her as she heard Daniel's brutal laugh.

'That's what they all say, darling.' The way he turned
the affectionate name into a scathing epithet made Jessica
flinch. 'That's what every woman since Eve has claimed
when things got a little too hot. Well, let me tell you

something, you try those cheap whore's tricks on any man and you'll find that's how he'll treat you too.'

Blind fury raged in Jessica's mind, obliterating rational thought. That 'cheap whore' incensed her, her anger combining with her own disgust at the way she had behaved to spark off a violent explosion.

'You bastard!' she yelled, her hand coming up to lash out at his face, wanting to wipe that darkly contemptuous expression from it.

But the blow never made contact. Daniel moved swiftly, hard fingers closing round her wrist, arresting the movement in mid-air.

'Yeah,' he drawled insolently, 'I'm a bastard—but think about your own behaviour and you'll see that you've nothing to be proud of.'

He waited a nicely calculated moment for his words to sink in, then, knowing from her face that the impulse to hit him had died, let her hand drop abruptly, his face twisting in distaste, as if he felt that simply to touch her had contaminated him.

'You can call me any name you like,' he went on, the controlled, steely hardness of his tone more frightening than if he had raged and shouted at her. 'And I'm quite sure your mind's buzzing with possible epithets right now—but while you're at it, try thinking of a few names for someone who uses her body to entice men into giving her what she wants—I'm sure you'll come up with a few, and you'll find they're not all that pretty either.'

'Jess?' Miriam's voice came as a shock. She had been so lost in her memories that she had forgotten where she was.

With a struggle Jessica dragged herself back to the present, focusing her mind with difficulty on what they had been talking about before.

'No, it's nothing whatsoever to do with what happened at college!' she declared emphatically; too emphatically, she realised as she heard the way her voice betrayed the disturbed state of her mind.

She felt as if she had been buried in the oozing, filthy slime of some stinking swamp, shame at the way she had behaved reviving painful echoes of how hard she had found it to face the following day. She had spent the night in terror of discovering that Daniel had spread the story of his conquest, that she might hear that scathing 'cheap whore's tricks' repeated over and over all round the college. She had even considered staying away, claiming to be ill, but she had known that if the story *had* spread everyone would guess at the reason for her absence. The only way was to face them at once and get it over with.

Now those memories were made all the worse by the recollection of the fact that, only three days before, she had actually reconsidered her attitude towards Daniel, believing her opinions to be too harshly coloured by what had happened nine years ago. For a short time she had been able to see him without prejudice, and something twisted deep inside her as she remembered how she had found herself liking the man he had become.

The man he had *appeared* to have become, Jessica told herself fiercely. Only a very short time afterwards she had come up against the truth about Daniel Tyson, and had found that in reality he hadn't changed at all.

'I don't think we're quite ready for the cabaret idea yet, Miriam,' she said, trying hard to make her voice sound calm and reasonable. 'This is the slow time of year with the Christmas season over and the cold, dark nights. No one wants to come out——'

'But that's precisely why we need a boost to our custom now! Just look at these bookings for the weekend.'

Miriam pulled the diary towards her and pointed to the relevant dates.

'Four tables on Saturday—ten people in all—and on Sunday only two. The place has been half-empty for weeks! A cabaret would bring people in, and Daniel made such an impact when he was here that everyone wants to see him again.'

Everyone in general, or you in particular? Jessica wondered, unable to erase the worried frown that creased her forehead.

'But it's more than that, isn't it?' Miriam had seen her expression. 'Just why don't you like Dan, Jess?'

'He——' Jessica began, then caught herself up. She couldn't reveal the truth; it wasn't her story to tell. Melvyn Tyson had been careful to keep the gory details from her, and it wouldn't be right to tell anyone else the story until she had let him know that Daniel was totally unrepentant. But she had to say something that would warn Miriam about the sort of man she was dealing with.

'He's a shallow, arrogant womaniser.' Her voice cracked unnervingly as she recalled how, in the pub, only minutes before his father's arrival, she had reviewed that opinion, believing it to be less than the truth—which it certainly was, though not in the way she had foolishly believed. 'Like a sailor, I'm sure he's got a girl in every port—and I know for a fact that he's messed around with at least one married woman.'

'Who told you that?'

Miriam's swift, defensive question aggravated Jessica's concern about her friend. Just how deeply was Miriam involved with Daniel Tyson?

'A—friend.' She couldn't say any more, though she dearly wished she could. 'Miriam, he's a thoroughly bad lot. I don't want anything to do with him.'

'You weren't so picky on Friday,' Miriam put in with an uncharacteristically caustic note.

'You know about that?' Jessica asked in surprise.

Her friend nodded. 'Dan told me. He said it didn't work out too well, though.'

That had to be the understatement of the year.

'He abandoned me in the Traveller's Rest car park. I had to get a taxi home.'

She preferred to forget about the long, disturbed walk she had had before she had finally exhausted herself enough to head for the nearest phone box to call that taxi.

'What did you argue about?'

Just what had Daniel told her? Not the truth; that much was obvious. Inspiration struck and she seized on the idea with gratitude.

'The way he treated his father.' That came near enough to what had happened to make her tone sound convincing. 'Melvyn Tyson came into the pub and Daniel simply cut him dead.'

'That doesn't surprise me.' Miriam's lack of concern left Jessica with the suspicion that Daniel had at least told her his version of his family history and the way his father had treated his mother, knowing of course that such a story, carefully slanted his way, would easily win her gentle, caring heart round to his side. But she'd bet every last penny she possessed that he'd left out the vital information about the way *he'd* behaved. 'Melvyn

Tyson's no angel, Jess. The woman he's married to now
is his——'

'Fourth wife. I know,' Jessica put in wearily. She was
thoroughly sick and tired of Daniel Tyson and anything
to do with him. She hadn't been able to get him out of
her mind since Friday—no, before then—since that first
evening when he had appeared in the restaurant. 'I liked
her.'

'So did Dan.' Miriam ignored her friend's stunned exclamation. 'He thinks she'll be good for his father.'

'He didn't stay around long enough to make any such
assessment!' Jessica commented tartly.

'No—he felt too uncomfortable.'

I'll bet he did! Jessica thought cynically. Even for a
heartless creature like Daniel Tyson, it must have been
a unique situation, meeting his father's new wife when
his own seduction of the previous one had probably been
the cause of the break-up of the earlier marriage in the
first place.

'Jess——' The earnest, appealing expression on
Miriam's face severely threatened Jessica's conviction
that she had no right to tell her friend the whole truth.
'Don't believe everything Melvyn Tyson tells you about
Daniel. He abandoned—— '

'I know about Daniel's mother, Miriam! But, believe
me, what I told you about him didn't come from his
father.'

If it had, then she might, like Miriam, be inclined to
have taken Daniel's side, Jessica reflected unhappily. It
was true that Melvyn Tyson wasn't completely innocent
in this affair, he had admitted as much himself. But there
could be no doubt at all about the veracity of the story
of Daniel and his stepmother, when confirmation of
those facts had come from Daniel himself. 'I'm sorry,

Miriam, but can we leave the subject now, please? I really must get on with these accounts. Alan Hampson's expecting them in his office first thing tomorrow and I'm not even half-way through.'

'All right, I'll leave you in peace,' Miriam agreed easily. 'But think about that cabaret idea, won't you? I'm sure it'd be a great success. Dan thought so too when I discussed it with him on Sunday. He's so keen on the idea that he's promised to keep the first two weeks in April free for us.'

Which was just the sort of remark that was guaranteed to destroy any chance of her making head or tail of the accounts, Jessica reflected wryly as the door closed behind Miriam. If her friend had already spoken to Daniel about the possible cabaret booking, wasn't he likely to turn up in Scarby in April anyway, no matter what she said about it? With a groan she buried her face in her hands, pushing her fingers through her hair, tangling its golden sleekness.

Oh, *why* had Daniel Tyson ever come back to Scarby? Why hadn't he gone away and stayed away, as she had believed he had when he had finally left the college to take up his place at university? She had never been so relieved to see the end of an academic year.

It had come as a great relief—and something of a surprise—to discover that, contrary to her expectations, no one seemed to have heard the story of her clash with Daniel; instead they had all been discussing another juicy bit of gossip, and Erica Stanton had made very sure that she was the one to tell Jessica.

'So much for your exaggerated sex appeal, Terry!' she had laughed. 'You were so sure of yourself—so convinced that Daniel Tyson would ask you to the disco! Well, you're losing your touch! The first thing Daniel did when he got here this morning was to walk straight over to Carly Alexander and ask *her* to go with him.'

If Daniel had meant to drive his point home, Jessica reflected, he couldn't have chosen a better way. Carly Alexander was one of the quietest, dullest girls in the college, and no one, not even her doting parents, could have denied the fact that she was painfully plain and undeniably fat. Her embarrassment at the thought of the humiliation of the previous night had been swept away under an avalanche of hurt pride, and she muddled through her classes with a maelstrom of anger rising inside her, so that when Daniel had caught up with her outside the college gates she had rounded on him savagely, lashing out in blind fury.

And now, sitting at her desk nine years later, Jessica felt even worse than she had at eighteen. Because now she knew the whole truth about that time. Now she knew that when Daniel Tyson had treated her so appallingly, calling her a cheap whore, telling her she disgusted him, he had probably already begun the seduction of his young stepmother and was possibly already sleeping with her in his father's house.

CHAPTER SEVEN

SUNDAY was an appalling day. From the moment Jessica woke up to find her bedroom flooded with an unearthly, greyish light, she knew that the snow which had been forecast had finally arrived with a vengeance. It continued to fall all morning, covering the streets and houses with a thick white blanket and turning familiar sights into unknown, alien territory. There was no chance of going anywhere, no hope of getting out of the house; the proposed visit to her parents had to be cancelled because of the dangers of travelling in such conditions and she could only be thankful that at least she did not have to go to work.

A phone call to Bill, who lived in the flat above the Jester, had brought the expected news that the few bookings they did have had already been cancelled because of the weather, and Jessica had decided that there was little point in opening up at all.

'I'll ring everyone and tell them not to bother going in,' she told Bill. 'We'll just have to hope that it's improved by tomorrow.'

She had just put the phone down on the last of the calls and was thinking longingly of a cup of coffee when the doorbell rang.

'Who can this be?' She spoke the question aloud in her amazement that anyone should venture out into the dangerous blizzard conditions outside. She shivered slightly; even though she was wearing a warm, soft blue jumper with toning cord jeans, the hall was still cold. Whoever was at the door would freeze if she didn't hurry.

A wild flurry of snow swept into her face as she opened the door, stinging her eyes so that she had to blink hard to focus. Her first, blurred impression was of a dark, powerful frame in a bulky padded jacket, but then her gaze went to a mane of rich chestnut hair and realisation set in fast.

'No!'

She reached for the door, meaning to slam it in his face, but his hand went out, arresting the movement easily.

'Jessica, please——' Daniel's voice was low and husky. 'We have to talk.'

'No, we don't!' Jessica declared rudely, struggling to resist the temptation to knock his hand from the door. 'I've said all I ever want to say to you and I——'

'I want to say I'm sorry.'

It was so unexpected that for a moment Jessica simply stared, meeting those clear eyes with total bemusement.

'I owe you an apology,' Daniel said quietly.

'Too damn right you do! You owe me an apology—and your father, and Kaye, and Miriam——'

'Miriam?'

The shocked surprise in his voice made her blink in confusion. The puzzled look in his eyes gave him a disturbingly vulnerable look that, even hating him as she did, she couldn't deny was distinctly appealing—but only for a moment. After that, common sense took charge once again.

'If you want to apologise to anyone, I think your father has first claim to that privilege—though in my opinion you're too late—nine years too late, to be precise.'

Her voice hardened as she remembered the phone call Melvyn Tyson had made to the Jester. He had been desperate to know if she had been able to talk to Daniel, if there was any hope of a reconciliation. It was cowardly, she knew, but she hadn't been able to tell him the truth. Instead she had said that by the time she had reached the car park Daniel had gone and she hadn't seen him since. She had known he hadn't believed her because he hadn't even asked why she hadn't gone back into the pub to tell him this, but had simply thanked her and put the phone down. How could she have told him that Daniel had declared the truth about his affair with his stepmother quite brazenly and unemotionally, without a hint of remorse?

'That's what I want to talk to you about.'

'There's nothing you can say.'

Inconsequentially, a part of Jessica's mind was registering how swiftly the snow was falling, piling up around the gate and on the roof of Daniel's car. The conditions really were atrocious. Daniel must be crazy to have ventured out in this; she was freezing already, just standing at the door.

'What possible justification can there be for...'

Her voice trailed off as she looked directly into Daniel's face, and immediately wished she hadn't. Why hadn't she noticed the lines around those tiger's eyes before?

No—unwanted, the thought came to her—they weren't tiger's eyes, not today. They were softer somehow, clouded as if by lack of sleep, and the shadows underneath them gave them a worryingly bruised look. Shaken by the way she had once more come close to feeling sympathy towards this man who she simply wanted to dislike and distrust, Jessica rushed on hastily.

'We have nothing to talk about, so I suggest you just get back in your car and take yourself off to——' A new thought struck her and she frowned confusedly. 'Where *have* you come from?'

'Doncaster.'

'*Doncaster?*' He must have been driving all morning—and she had told her staff not even to risk the journey into town! 'You've come all that way in this?'

Daniel's wide mouth twisted into a wry, rather shame-faced grin that gave his face a new, boyish look.

'I know it was crazy, but I couldn't get away before—and I only finally made up my mind last night. I've spent all week thinking about it, wondering if it was better to leave things alone. I had to come in person—I was sure it was no good phoning. I thought you'd slam the receiver down when you knew it was me.'

'You're damn right I would!'

She tried to make it sound sharp and definite, but the truth was that she was having difficulty maintaining her hostility towards Daniel. Her fingers were like blocks of ice on the door-handle, and she felt that if she didn't move soon her feet would freeze to the floor—and she at least was inside, protected from the worst of the blizzard. Daniel was out in the full force of it.

Jessica looked at him reluctantly, seeing how his shoulders were hunched against the driving wind, his hands thrust deep into his pockets. His bright hair was plastered against his head, the melting snow turning it into dripping tendrils around his head. As she watched, a drop of icy water detached itself and trickled down towards the corner of his eye, and he shook his head to remove it, stamping his feet to clear them of the snow that was piling up around his ankles.

'You've driven all the way from Doncaster in the worst blizzard for years?' She was unable to erase the shaken note from her voice. *'Why?'*

Hazel eyes locked with hers. Daniel's frank, open gaze twisted something deep inside her so that she shifted uneasily from one foot to another.

'To see you.'

That wonderful voice was low and intent, and there was no trace of the smiling charm she had believed was all artifice, aimed at winning over the gullible, only a direct and thoroughly disconcerting honesty. Unnervingly, all Jessica could think of was that moment on the moors when she had seen him with eyes unclouded by the past, and acknowledged that he was one of the most attractive men she had ever met. Even now, with his dripping hair and his skin grey with the cold, he exerted a rugged, magnetic appeal that aimed straight at some inner core of her being like an arrow flying towards the gold in the centre of the target.

'Jessica—please——'

It would have taken a far harder heart than Jessica possessed to resist the appeal in that 'please', and before she had rationally made the decision she found she had taken a couple of steps backwards, opening the door wider.

'You'd better come in.'

Ambiguous feelings made the words come out stiffly and grudgingly, and she took another hasty step to the side to avoid touching him as he moved into the hall. She had had to let him in, she rationalised; she couldn't have left a dog standing outside in this weather any longer, but that didn't mean she wanted any contact with him.

Jessica turned from closing the door to find Daniel standing just behind her, watching her closely. His silence aggravated her uncomfortable feelings, increasing them one hundredfold. It was one thing to act on a humanitarian impulse and invite him in, quite another to be alone with him in her flat like this. The couple who lived upstairs were away for the weekend, so there was no one else in the house, and she didn't trust Daniel Tyson one little bit.

'You'd better take your coat off,' she said gruffly, resorting to conventional courtesy to cover her unease, though deep down she felt that Daniel didn't deserve even such minimal consideration.

'Is it worth it?'

If the question surprised her, the voice in which it was uttered rocked her sense of reality. Daniel sounded hesitant, uncertain, almost as if he was afraid of how she would react—none of which fitted with the Daniel she thought she knew. *That* Daniel would have sauntered into her home as if he owned the place, removing his coat and settling himself in a chair without waiting to be asked.

'The least I can do is to offer you a cup of coffee. You must be frozen.'

A brief smile flashed on and off like a neon sign.

'That's an understatement,' Daniel said drily, shrugging himself out of his jacket. He grimaced as another drop of water trickled down his face and wiped it away with an impatient movement. 'Do you think you could lend me a towel? He brushed at his face again and surveyed the back of his hand with a rueful expression. 'I'd prefer not to drip all over your carpet.'

'My landlord's carpet,' Jessica corrected jerkily. Without the bulky coat, Daniel should have seemed smaller, less imposing; instead, she found herself highly sensitive to his forceful physical presence, the strongly built frame in a cream Shetland sweater and dark brown cord jeans seeming to fill the small hallway, making her feel as if she were trapped in the confined space with some powerful jungle cat. Her pulse had started to race unevenly, so that her voice sounded breathless and shaken. 'I haven't been able to afford a place of my own yet—all the profits had to be ploughed back into the Jester. Anyway——' She wished he wouldn't watch her like that. There was no way he could be unaware of the disturbed state of her feelings which was betrayed by the rapid rise and fall of her chest, the heightened colour in her cheeks. '—I don't think a few drops of water could make it much worse than it is.'

'True.' Daniel surveyed the worn green carpet consideringly. 'Even so,' he added, 'it's still rather better than the carpet in my place.'

His words sparked off a whole new train of thought in Jessica's mind. Somehow she had never really thought of Daniel as having a home. He seemed more like the eternal wanderer, a travelling man, rootless, no ties. Now she tried to picture him in a shabby flat in London, and found that the image intensified her ambiguous feelings about him.

She was forced to remember the conversation they had had about the challenge of starting out in a new venture, the empathetic understanding Daniel had showed of the excitement and enjoyment that came from putting up with discomforts, economies and hard work which were all worth while because of the ultimate goal towards which they were aiming. Daniel could have had a successful career in law or even politics, but he had given that up in order to work for the aims that were personal to him, and that was something she deeply admired.

'Comedy doesn't bring in a good living?'

She had doubts about the way she had phrased the question, her conflicting inner feelings making it sound slightly awkward, perhaps even critical. But Daniel answered equably, his eyes meeting hers directly.

'I'm certainly not amassing any fortunes, but it's coming. And I have plans—hopes——'

The oblique comment was intriguing. In any other circumstances Jessica would have liked to ask more, to find out what those plans were, but a sudden rush of awareness of exactly who this man was, the memory of the dark secret she knew about him, dried the question in her throat and had her saying instead, 'I'll get a towel. You go into the lounge and thaw out—there's a fire in there.'

By the time she had made coffee and brought it through from the kitchen, Daniel was standing at the window staring out at the whirling snow that made it impossible to see more than a yard or two before him. His hair had been roughly dried, and, although still several shades darker than its natural rich colour, showed a tendency to curve into waves in the warmth of the room.

'I'm going to have to dig my car out when I go,' he said, turning as Jessica placed the tray on a coffee-table. 'I just hope I can make it to Sheffield tomorrow—there'll be hell to pay if I don't get there on time.'

'It must be a lonely life, always on the move.'

Jessica's response came stiffly. She didn't want to make polite conversation with this man; what she wanted was for him to tell her what he had come to say and be on his way. No, she amended hastily, what she *really* wanted was for him to drink his coffee and go without another word. She didn't want to hear what he had to say, didn't want anything from him except that he got out of her life and left her in peace. She hadn't been able to settle to anything since he had strolled into the Jester that Monday morning—was it really only two weeks ago? She felt as if she'd lived through several lifetimes since then.

'Lonely?' Daniel mused, considering the word. 'No—solitary perhaps, but not lonely. Lonely was how I felt when I left Scarby.'

For which he only had himself to blame, Jessica was tempted to retort, but for the sake of peace she bit back the words and concentrated on pouring the coffee as if her life depended on not spilling a single drop. She couldn't cope with any more battles with Daniel.

'Milk and sugar?'

Glancing up as she spoke, she caught the way his mouth twisted at the cold, tight sound of her voice. Well, what did he expect? Her better nature might have forced her to take pity on him, let him into the house like a stray dog caught in the snowstorm, but that didn't mean she had to be polite to him.

'Neither, thanks.'

To her surprise, nothing of her own sharpness was echoed in Daniel's tone. Did he, too, want to avoid any confrontation? From what she knew of him, that seemed extremely unlikely.

'Anyway,' Daniel went on, continuing the previous conversation, 'it's a life that suits me.'

'I'll bet it does!' This time the words would not be bitten back. 'And I'd be willing to lay odds that "solitary" is not the word to describe it, either.'

'And just what is that supposed to mean?'

Daniel had come to sit down as he spoke, picking up the mug she had filled for him and regarding her steadily across the top of it. As her grey eyes met his hazel ones and she saw the light of battle in them, Jessica reflected that at last the real Daniel Tyson was back. The subdued, strangely hesitant man she had opened the door to had put her off balance for a while, but *this* Daniel was one she recognised.

'Work it out for yourself,' she snapped.

'Oh, come on, Mystery, that isn't like you.' The glint had brightened to a mocking gleam, making Jessica's skin prickle in irritation as she gritted her teeth in reaction to that taunting 'Mystery'. 'You've never held back on your opinion of me before, so why start now?'

'Do I need to elaborate?' Jessica injected as much biting sarcasm into her voice as she could. 'You can't pretend not to know what I mean, and I'm sure there must be hundreds of women in towns all over the country who would be able to testify to the fact that your nights at least haven't been exactly *solitary* while you've been on the road.'

The smile that curved his lips was hard and bitter, and she shivered as she saw that it didn't touch his eyes which were just like amber chips of ice.

'I've told you already that hundreds is an exaggeration—way over the top,' he said in a coldly reasonable tone that was all the more worrying in the way it revealed none of the anger she could see in his eyes, over which he was clearly imposing a ruthless control. 'I'm no saint, but neither am I criminally irresponsible or possessed of a death wish, which I'd have to be if I indulged in the sort of indiscriminate sexual behaviour you're implying. And if we're trading insults, perhaps

you ought to make sure that your own slate is clean
before you start slinging accusations around.'

'My—I——' Jessica spluttered, unable to string two
coherent words together in her anger. 'What *are* you
talking about?'

'You, Mystery,' Daniel drawled lazily, leaning back in
his chair. 'I'm talking about you. I know you, remember. I saw you almost every day for nine months—
and I knew your reputation.'

'Rep—reputation!'

Jessica's head was spinning. Whatever she had
expected when she had opened the door to find him
standing there, it certainly hadn't been this. Hadn't he
said something about an apology, or had she misheard
him? Or had he simply said that in order to lull her into
a false sense of security so that she would invite him in?
Either way, one thing was sure—in this particular fight,
the gloves were well and truly off.

'Did you ever know any of your nicknames, I
wonder?' Daniel's voice was deceptively gentle as he
stared down into his coffee-mug—too gentle, Jessica
thought on a *frisson* of apprehension. The mood he was
in, he clearly had no intention of pulling any punches.
'Did you ever hear of Terry the Tease, or——'

'*No!*'

His head came up at her exclamation, and his smile
was a slow, sardonic curl of his lips that she hated on
sight.

'No, I don't suppose you did. But, believe me, that
was one of the more polite names. You thought you were
the Queen Bee, didn't you? You had every male in the
place buzzing round you and you loved it. They weren't
people to you, they were just trophies—notches on your
belt.'

'No.'

This time it was just a low whisper, as Jessica closed her eyes to shut out that taunting, goading smile. But she couldn't block out his words, and they echoed over and over inside her head.

Terry the Tease. Was that really how it had seemed? Seeing things through Daniel's eyes, she was forced to admit that perhaps it was. She *had* flirted indiscriminately, determined to enjoy herself, but it had all been just in a spirit of fun—or had it?

Remembering the way she had felt about the Christmas disco, her determination to be the first girl to date Daniel Tyson, the boy everyone wanted to be seen with, Jessica was forced to rethink rapidly, and with a jarring sense of shock she suddenly saw herself as everyone else must have seen her, as a vain, self-centred little madam who thought the world was her oyster—with herself as the pearl at its centre.

'And you haven't stopped now, have you?' that hard voice went on. 'You're still stringing the poor fools along.'

'*What?*' Jessica's eyes flew open, meeting his steely hard ones with a clash that she could almost hear. 'I don't know what you mean!'

'Don't you? I saw you that Monday in the restaurant. You were with some poor sucker——'

'John,' Jessica croaked, remembering.

She could see the scene in her mind: John trying to persuade her to go to the theatre with him—Daniel's arrival—that foolish business of the tie. At the time she had sensed a strongly controlled hostility in Daniel's demeanour but, thinking about it later, she had assumed he had been angry because he had known very well who she was, nothing more.

'Mr Bennett—your *guest*.' Daniel's intonation loaded the word with contempt. 'The poor fool was crazy about you, anyone could see that, and you were leading him on, promising everything but giving nothing.'

The savagely cynical words bit into Jessica's nerves like burning acid, and she wanted to scream, to shout, to tell him to go to hell and stay there, but she forced herself to review the situation rationally, recalling how John had taken her hand just at the moment that Daniel had arrived in the restaurant.

Seen through prejudiced eyes, that scene could have been interpreted exactly as Daniel had said—and he *was* prejudiced against her. If her reputation at college had been as bad as he claimed—hot colour flooded her cheeks at the thought—then he would naturally have assumed that she was still the same selfish flirt he had known all those years ago.

Swallowing hard, Jessica gathered together the shattered remnants of her composure and tried to speak in a calm, controlled voice.

'John Bennett is a friend who has just been through a particularly nasty divorce. He loved his wife very much and was devastated when she left him. Any attraction he feels towards me is on the rebound from her, nothing more. I felt it was kinder to make it clear where I stood from the start, rather than give him any false hopes. If I had agreed to go out with him, it would just have been out of friendship, and when he came to his senses he would have felt patronised and very foolish indeed.'

She risked a glance into those burning amber eyes and immediately regretted it when she saw the fierce intensity with which they were fixed on her face, clearly noting every fleeting emotion that crossed it.

Did he believe a word she said? She didn't know; his expression was closed and unreadable, it was like looking into the carved face of a marble statue. An unnerving flash of insight made her pause to wonder why it mattered whether he believed her or not. She didn't need this man's approval, didn't care what he thought of her! But, strangely, this declaration rang disturbingly hollow. She *wanted* Daniel to believe her, and she wanted to convince him that she had changed, that she was no longer the shallow adolescent he had first known. Drawing a deep breath, she forced herself to go on.

'Perhaps I could have been kinder—more delicate— but I'd just been through the break-up of a relationship myself...'

She worked hard on her voice, and was pleased to find that no trace of anything that could be interpreted as self-pity coloured it.

'I was feeling pretty——'

Jessica hunted for the right word, supremely conscious of that probing hazel gaze that made her feel like a defendant in the dock, facing a particularly hostile prosecuting counsel. The worrying recollection that Daniel had studied law gave an added edge to the need to express herself clearly.

'—pretty raw and unsettled,' she managed eventually. 'Jack and I had been together for some time, and the break-up came as a shock. I never meant to hurt John,' she went on earnestly, leaning towards Daniel in her concern to get the truth through to him. 'If my attitude seemed hard, it was only because I felt I had to be cruel in order to be kind.'

I rest my case, she thought as she finished speaking. There was nothing more she could say. All she could do now was wait to find out what verdict Daniel would come to. Unconsciously she crossed her fingers superstitiously.

Daniel didn't speak for what seemed like a very long time, his silence stretching Jessica's already tight nerves to breaking-point, and when at last he did comment, what he said was unexpected.

'Jack?' He made the name a question. 'That was the name...'

He let the sentence trail off, and Jessica swallowed hard to ease an uncomfortably dry throat as she recalled the circumstances under which he had heard Jack's name before, on the night at the theatre when he had kissed her in the car park.

'I think I've jumped to some rather hasty conclusions.' Daniel's concession was the last thing she had expected, and the rush of relief it brought loosened her frozen tongue.

'Which was only to be expected from what you knew of me before,' she said, wanting to offer an equal concession on her own part. 'I—I was pretty thoughtless in those days, vain and self-centred. Looking back, I can see that and I have to admit that I'm not proud of the way I behaved. It's too late to apologise to any of the boys I messed around, I know, but I *am* sorry if I treated them badly. Can you believe that?'

'If you can do the same for me.'

'What?' Jessica's voice betrayed her confusion as her eyes flew to Daniel's, seeing how, under the heavy lids, they were dark and sombre like shadows in a forest.

'I came here to apologise, Jessica. I fully intended that it would be the first thing I said to you, but I—got a little lost along the way.'

Jessica could hardly believe what she was hearing or the tone in which he had spoken—all aggression, all mockery gone from his voice. Lost, he had said, a word she would have never associated with Daniel Tyson, and his tone had once more been touched with that hint of uncertainty and hesitation.

'I lied to you,' Daniel said as she stared at him in blank confusion. 'No——' He lifted a hand as if to erase the words. 'Not lied—I told you the exact truth, but not all of it.'

'I don't understand.'

Daniel pushed a hand roughly through his almost dry hair, ruffling its damp sleekness, and inconsequentially Jessica couldn't help noticing how the tousled effect softened his face, making it look less harsh and unapproachable, infinitely more human.

'I said that my father threw me out because he found me in bed with my stepmother—what I should have said was that he found *her* in bed with *me*.'

He paused for a moment to let his words sink in, and Jessica needed that time to consider what he had said. 'He found *her* in bed with *me*'—such a tiny change, but that slight rearrangement of the vital words made all the difference in the world, one that caused ripples to spread out from it as if from a stone that had been thrown into a pond. There *was* a possible explanation for the way he had behaved, after all—if she could believe it. Recalling how she had wanted that explanation so much a week ago, Jessica bit her lip, not knowing what to say.

'I was barely twenty.' Daniel had caught the small, revealing movement and intuitively interpreted it as betraying her need to know more. 'My mother had just died.'

His voice was flat, emotionless, but the shadows in his eyes revealed how hard he found it to speak of those times, and Jessica's heart twisted in instinctive sympathy. There wasn't a trace of self-pity in his tone, he was giving her the facts, nothing more, but, putting herself in his place, she could feel for the vulnerable youth—little more than a boy—he had been then.

'She was never very strong, and she'd had to work desperately hard to bring me up alone. My father——'

The muscles in his jaw tightened, compressing the wide mouth into a thin, hard line, and he bent his head, staring fixedly at his tightly clasped hands.

'My father married her before he started to achieve any sort of success, but by the time I was born his fame had gone to his head. He had an affair with one of his co-stars in the show, divorced my mother and married her. It only lasted a couple of years and when *they* were divorced she demanded a large settlement that meant there was very little left over for my mother.'

Daniel's head came up swiftly, his eyes blazing into Jessica's.

'She never asked for anything anyway. She had too much pride. She worked herself into the ground to support me, making sure I lacked for nothing. She went without, never had any luxuries——'

'And you loved her very much,' Jessica put in quietly when the raw-toned words were choked off. There was no doubt about that; it was written all over his face.

'Yes.' The fingers of Daniel's clasped hands tightened until the knuckles showed white. 'And I hated and despised my father for the way he'd treated her. By now he was a big name, his picture was often in the papers, so I knew when he started being seen with Charlotte— a girl who was young enough to be his daughter. She was only five years older than me.'

Daniel reached for his mug, draining what was left of his coffee, and drew a deep breath, as if steeling himself to continue. Jessica waited in silence, knowing he had to tell this his own way. The time for any questions or comment on her part would come later.

'When I was seventeen Mother discovered she had cancer. For the last eighteen months of her life she needed constant nursing, so the only logical thing was that I should leave school to look after her. She was against the idea—she wanted me to do my exams, go to university, but we couldn't afford any professional help, so there was no alternative. But Mother was determined that I wouldn't be held back, and when she knew she'd very little time left she swallowed her pride and wrote to my father. He offered to let me go and live with him after she died so that I could get a place at the local college, finish my exams.'

Daniel sighed heavily, pushing both hands through his dark hair.

'I didn't want to do it. I didn't know the man—he meant nothing to me. But Mother made me promise I'd give it a try, at least until I'd got my A levels and a place at university. So I came here——'

No wonder he'd been so withdrawn, such a loner, Jessica reflected, sympathy wrenching at her heart. He'd just lost the mother he loved and admired; he'd been uprooted from his home and the life he knew, and he was living with a father who was a stranger to him, and a twenty-five-year-old stepmother.

'My father wasn't what I'd expected. I'd built up a picture of some appalling ogre in my mind, instead I found a very likeable man who'd made a mess of things and was now, belatedly, trying to put things right. But Charlie——'

Daniel's face hardened, becoming a cold, remote mask.

'Charlie was a different kettle of fish altogether. She'd married a star, but the series had been axed because of a drop in popularity. My father was almost fifty, he didn't need to work—his second wife had married again and he was no longer supporting her. He'd always dreamed of retiring to the country, so he'd bought a house here and was quite content. But Charlie was a big city girl. She wanted the social life, the publicity she'd known, the bright lights. She was also an inveterate flirt.'

Jessica caught her breath sharply as she saw the way his story was heading.

'She made a play for you?'

Daniel nodded grimly.

'At first I thought she was just being friendly—and I'll admit I welcomed it. I didn't know anyone else in the area and she kept offering to take me out, show me places. My father was pleased to see us getting on so well, so he never interfered. In fact, he actively encouraged it. But when I realised there was more to it than just friendliness I tried to back out—fast. I did everything I could to show her I wasn't interested. I worked late at college, tried to avoid being alone with her, but she was impervious to hints, even to blunt warnings to get lost. She kept coming to my room, trying to touch me, kiss me——'

He laughed, that dark, cynical laugh Jessica hated so much, but now she felt she understood something of what lay behind it, and that made it infinitely worse.

'Christmas was a wonderful time for her. For weeks beforehand she had mistletoe pinned up all over the house, and she grabbed at every chance to get me underneath it.'

Christmas! Jessica sat up sharply, feeling as if someone had suddenly switched on a light that illuminated a dark corner of the past so brightly that her mind reeled.

'The Christmas disco——' she said hoarsely, her throat painfully dry. At home he had been subjected to this harassment by his stepmother, and at college she, Jessica, had been doing very much the same sort of thing.

For a second Daniel looked blank, then he nodded slowly.

'The Christmas disco,' he echoed dully. 'I'm afraid you caught the backlash from what was happening at home, and I'm sorry. The things I said to you were the things I wanted to say to Charlie but couldn't because she have reported them straight to my father—carefully tailored to fit her version of events, with me as the villain, of course—and I was just beginning to form some sort of relationship with him.'

His eyes went to Jessica's, honest, open, concealing nothing.

'And by then I *wanted* that relationship; I'd have done anything to make it work. But it was Charlie, not you, I was attacking.'

And that Jessica could understand. He must have felt as if he was living with a keg of gunpowder, its fuse lit and burning away slowly—and her actions had brought about the final explosion.

'I'm sorry too,' she said softly. 'I didn't know—but that's no excuse. I was way out of line.'

For a moment a brief flicker of humour curled the corners of Daniel's mouth upwards.

'In any other circumstances I might have enjoyed it,' he said with a boyishly lop-sided grin. 'I wasn't exactly immune to you—unlike Charlie, who left me completely cold. But you had a reputation as a flirt—a mankiller—and I already had more on my plate than I could handle.'

'I must have seemed like another Charlie, coming on so strongly.'

Try as she might, Jessica couldn't smooth out the unevenness in her voice that was the result of that casually spoken, 'I wasn't exactly immune to you,' which had made her heart leap in unexpected pleasure.

'But you weren't married to my father, and that made all the difference. When I calmed down I was disgusted with the way I'd treated you and I wanted to explain——'

'But I didn't give you a chance.' Honesty forced Jessica to add, 'But you taught me a valuable lesson that day. Afterwards I realised that I'd only myself to blame, and I never behaved like that again. So tell me the rest,' she added, when Daniel didn't speak. 'What happened in the end?'

She wished the question hadn't had to be asked when she saw the light fade from his eyes and the cold, remote mask slide down over his face once again. She could guess what had happened, but she needed to hear it from Daniel himself.

'I managed to keep Charlie at a distance for the next couple of months.' Daniel spoke slowly, with obvious reluctance. 'She and my father went away on holiday, which helped, but then in the summer she started chasing me again. My father hadn't been well, and apparently their sex-life was non-existent, which didn't suit Charlie. On the day I got my exam results I went out with some friends to celebrate, and I got back very late. My father was in London and wasn't expected back until the next day, but Charlie was in the house—asleep, I thought.'

His face darkened, that cynical twist distorting his mouth.

'I was wrong—she was very much awake, and she'd been waiting for me. I'd just got into bed when she came into the room. She said she wanted to congratulate me, and as I wasn't exactly sober I didn't resist when she kissed me. I was pretty bloody naïve, because I thought that was all she wanted—but then she said she wanted to congratulate me *properly* and got into bed with me. That was when my father came home.'

'But didn't you explain?'

'Jess, I was drunk. I wasn't thinking straight. As soon as I saw his face I knew he'd got me marked down as the villain of the piece. He was besotted with Charlie, blind to all her faults. He'd judged me and found me guilty before I had time to speak. He called me every name under the sun, said I was no son of his, and told me to get out of his house right there and then.'

'Why didn't you say anything?'

The twist to Daniel's mouth became more pronounced.

'Oh, I said plenty—none of it very wise. I lost my temper too, and I dragged up the past and flung it in his face. I told him how I'd hated him for what he'd done to my mother, how I'd never wanted to come and live with him in the first place——'

Jessica could picture the scene, the two of them snapping and snarling like wounded animals, hiding their pain behind a mask of anger, and in her mind she could hear Melvyn Tyson's voice saying, 'We're too much alike—both plagued with an excess of stubborn pride.'

'Charlie had run out and gone to her bedroom—apparently in tears—and after a time my father went after her. When he'd gone I packed my bags and left. I haven't been back since.'

The last bleak words came starkly, but Jessica barely heard them. In her thoughts she was listening to his voice as she had heard it only a short time before. 'Lonely was how I felt when I left Scarby.' At the time she hadn't fully understood what he meant, but now she did and her heart ached in sympathy.

'Daniel, your father wants you back, he told me so. Perhaps he wouldn't have listened to you then, but he will now. Don't let the past keep you apart; it'll only hurt both of you! And Kaye would help—she's nothing like Charlie.'

'I know. You only have to look at her to know that she loves him.' Daniel sighed despondently. 'I handled that meeting very badly—messed it up completely—and I've been cursing myself ever since. I knew that if I came back to Scarby there was every chance I'd meet up with my father some time, but I didn't expect it to happen then. Kaye was a surprise too. When I heard that Father had married again, I expected someone like Charlie. He was always a fool about women—a sucker for a pretty face.'

The wry grin that softened his expression told Jessica that there was still a chance for Daniel and his father. If she could only find a way to get them back together...

'But there was something else I couldn't handle that day, something that affected my judgement so that I wasn't thinking any more clearly than the first time.'

Jessica frowned, puzzled. 'What was that?'

'Can't you guess?'

Daniel's eyes locked with hers, his voice deepening, becoming huskily intent.

'I couldn't think straight at all that day because of you.'

CHAPTER EIGHT

'ME?'

Twice Jessica tried to form the word, and each time her voice failed her. On the third attempt she managed a feeble croak that brought a wry smile to Daniel's mouth.

'Is it so very hard to believe? Or is the idea totally repulsive to you?'

'No—not repulsive.' Something strange had happened to her breathing; it was fast and shallow, making her feel worryingly light-headed.

'I never meant it to happen, you know.' A touch of self-deprecation shaded Daniel's tone. 'The first time I saw you again I thought you'd grown into a stunning woman, but you seemed cold—hard—and I was convinced you were still stringing men along as you'd done at college. I didn't even want to like you, but I found I was drawn to you. I couldn't get you out of my mind. That day on the moors I found that my whole opinion of you was changing—I liked your company, your honesty, I wanted to talk and talk and never stop—then my father and Kaye appeared and—well, I just blew a fuse. I didn't know if I was on my head or my heels. I couldn't cope with all three of you.'

Once more his strong hands raked through the bright chestnut hair.

'Seeing Dad like that, it was like being back in the past. All I could see was his face on that last night—the anger and disgust that had filled it—and when you came

to me in the car park and told me you knew what had
happened, I knew he'd told you, that it was still the first
thing in his mind when he thought of me. I just blew
up, I lost my temper as stupidly and blindly as I had
done nine years ago. Later, when I came to my senses,
I cursed myself for being all sorts of a bloody fool. I've
spent this last week wondering what to do. The number
of times I've picked up the phone to ring you——'

A shake of his head revealed his confusion, and when
Jessica looked into his eyes she saw that they were no
longer that clear, bright hazel, but dark and deep, only
a rim of gold showing at the edge of his pupils.

'Jessica——'

Jessica knew what was coming, and she wasn't ready
to handle it. She had moved from loathing this man,
detesting and despising everything he was, to a better
understanding of him—but it was all too new, too fragile.
It had all happened in the space of less than an hour,
and she needed time to adjust, to absorb what she had
learned before she could decide if she was ready to move
on to anything else.

'Daniel, no——' Getting to her feet in agitation, she
moved round the room like a restless, unsettled cat. 'We
have to talk about your father.'

'I don't want to talk about him!'

The explosive exclamation brought Daniel to his feet,
violent emotion showing in his eyes. Then, with a savage
curse, he slammed one fist into the palm of the other
hand.

'Hell, yes I do!' The look he turned on Jessica was
filled with such a lost loneliness that she wanted to run
to his side, enfold him in her arms. 'Jess—what do I
do?'

'*Go* to him!' Total confidence infused Jessica's words. 'Go to him and tell him everything you've told me. He'll listen,' she rushed on as she saw him shake his head in denial. 'I know he will. He told me he'd do anything to put things right. And, Daniel——' It was amazing how easily his name came to her tongue now, the stiffly formal 'Mr Tyson' buried under all they had shared. 'Your father didn't tell me about Charlie, he didn't even mention her. I found out about that from someone else— someone who only knew the story because your father got very drunk and let it out.'

Was there the light of hope in his eyes? She prayed there was, but she couldn't be sure. Instead, he looked like a man being torn in two by conflicting loyalties.

'Your father needs you.' She drove home her advantage as forcefully as she could. 'He's been ill——' she reminded him.

She saw Daniel's face change as he came to a decision.

'Where's my coat?' He was heading towards the door as he spoke.

He was doing the right thing, the only thing, every instinct told Jessica that, so why did she suddenly feel so terribly lost, as if something very precious had just been snatched away from her?

She followed Daniel into the hall where, still with his coat only half on and completely unfastened, he yanked open the door. The howling gale that swept into the hallway rocked him back on his heels.

'You can't drive in this!' She could barely see the end of the path, and his car was just a larger, more substantial mass of white in the whirling blur. 'You'll kill yourself!'

'Jess, I have to.'

He was actually prepared to risk his life in the blizzard. She saw the determination stamped hard on his features, the need burning in his eyes, but she couldn't let him go.

'Daniel, no!'

Exerting every ounce of strength she possessed, Jessica put her weight against the door and slammed it shut. In the silence that followed she couldn't look into his face. The fear that had gripped her when she thought of the dangers he would face in such appalling conditions still had her in its grasp, and she found she was trembling all over in reaction.

'It's been *nine years*——'

Daniel's low voice penetrated the fog that seemed to have clouded her mind, and she gave herself a vicious mental shake to clear her thoughts. She understood and sympathised with how he felt, but she could never live with herself it she let him expose himself to the hazards involved in driving to his father's house in this weather.

'Jess, *please...*'

Turning slowly, Jessica took a deep breath, not knowing what she could say. But then her gaze fell on the telephone and immediately everything became very clear and very simple.

She knew the number off by heart. It had buzzed around in her head all week, reminding her of her promise, tormenting her with the way she had avoided telling Melvyn Tyson how completely she had failed to carry it out. Slowly she lifted the receiver and dialled.

'Kaye? It's Jessica Terry. Is your husband there? Daniel's here with me—he wants to speak to his father.'

Then, ducking her head because the expression on Daniel's face would be too private, too personal for her to intrude on, she thrust the receiver at the man standing beside her and fled into the living-room, closing the door firmly behind her.

It was a long time before Daniel came back into the room, and when he did she scarcely recognised him. It was as if the burden that had been lifted from his shoulders had taken years from him, too, so that she could almost believe that it was the twenty-year-old Daniel who stood before her, except that at twenty he had never looked so completely happy, and had never had that glowing light in his eyes.

'All right?' she asked softly and unnecessarily, and he simply nodded, the inner glow that transformed his face bringing her out of her seat to catch hold of his hands and squeeze them hard. 'I knew it would be! Oh, Dan, I'm so happy for you!'

Her heart seemed to stop as she heard what she had said, the softening of his name reminding her of how on more than one occasion he had used the gentler, more affectionate 'Jess', and suddenly it was as if time had stood still and there was only the two of them, suspended in this very special moment.

'I can't thank you enough——' Daniel's voice was hoarsely hesitant, and as their eyes met she read his intention clearly in their depths.

He just wanted to thank her, she told herself, that was all, and she met his lips softly, willingly, letting herself be drawn into his arms without a murmur of protest.

She thought it would be different this time. Without the fear and the hatred that had complicated matters before, she believed she would be able to accept his kiss in the spirit in which it was given and nothing more, but the truth was that from the moment Daniel's lips touched hers she wasn't thinking at all, but simply feeling.

His mouth was tentative at first, as if he feared she might pull away from him, but then, sensing her acceptance, he pressed his lips insistently on hers, prising them apart, his kiss becoming deeper, more possessive, awakening an aching hunger deep inside her.

She *wanted* this! Oh, how she wanted it! Her whole body longed for his touch, a tiny, gasping cry of satisfaction escaping her as she felt his hands slide down her back and under the blue jumper she wore. His caresses burned along her skin, making her writhe against him, bringing her hips and legs into tantalising contact with the hardness of his own, the barrier of their clothes suddenly a source of painful frustration. Her fingers were busy with the buttons on the shirt he wore under his sweater, their impatient movements freezing when Daniel's hands closed over her breasts, sparking off a sensual explosion that ripped through her, making her cry aloud in delight.

'Jess.' Her name was a husky whisper in her ear. 'Jess, this is how it should be—the two of us together——'

What had happened to her fears, her uncertainty? They no longer existed; nothing existed beyond herself and Daniel and the private world which enclosed them. Daniel's kisses grew more urgent, more demanding, and Jessica responded eagerly as the hunger inside her grew to a soaring, raging need that could not be controlled.

She was swung up into Daniel's arms, his mouth never leaving hers as he kicked open the door to her bedroom and carried her through, releasing her only for a moment as he let her gently down on to the bed.

'This *is* what you want?'

Did he still doubt it? Jessica could find no words to answer him, but instinct told her how to respond as she held out her arms, and with a thick, rough sound in his throat he came swiftly to lie beside her, easing her sweater from her and lowering his head to rest it against her breasts. The burnished chestnut of his hair glowed against her pale skin, and Jessica lifted tentative fingers to stroke it softly. She couldn't believe what was happening to her. It seemed so unreal—so dreamlike—that this man, whom she had once hated so much, could make her feel so wonderfully wanted, so desired, so supremely, totally female.

Her thoughts shattered, her fingers clenching in the bright, silky strands, as Daniel's mouth found one nipple and closed over it, tugging softly. Her blood seemed to be molten lava in her veins, burning at white heat so that she stirred restlessly, arching her body against his, his name a constant, incoherent murmur on her lips as desire knifed through her with a pleasure so intense it was almost a pain.

'You're beautiful,' Daniel muttered against her breasts, the warm, featherlight touch of his breath on her sensitised flesh making her gasp her pleasure out loud. 'So, so beautiful! Dear heaven, Jess, I've wanted this for so long.'

And she had too, Jessica realised with a convulsive shudder of awareness. From that first moment he had kissed her all those years ago, even while she had believed she hated him, this had been her destiny. It had been written into the script of her life, inevitable as drawing breath.

Impatient hands, clumsy with need, found buttons, fastenings, until their clothes lay discarded around them, their movements blind, instinctive, all their concentration centred on each other, oblivious to time or place. Every touch of Daniel's lips and fingers triggered responses that were even more delightful, more mind-shattering, the crescendo of longing reaching its peak as she felt the hard weight of his strong body cover hers.

But even through the fire of sensation that raged in her Jessica knew she was not alone in her passion. Daniel was clinging to her as fiercely as she to him, his uncharacteristic lack of control sweeping her along on a tide of ecstasy, carrying her with him into a fiery maelstrom that seemed to blow her mind apart.

Slowly, very slowly, the blaze of satisfaction receded, becoming a gradually diminishing glow that faded to still-warm embers, leaving them both spent and consumed, and as Jessica lay lost in wonder at all that had happened she felt that a new understanding had been forged in the heat of their passion, one that promised a glorious beginning and the hope of greater happiness to come.

'When I came here today, I thought I had nothing.' Daniel's voice was husky and shaken as he took her head between both his hands and brushed delicate kisses over her face. 'My father—you—I thought I'd lost it all for good. Instead, I find I have almost everything I've ever wanted.'

'Me, too,' Jessica murmured, smiling in lazily satiated contentment. 'Me, too.'

It was only very much later that the revealing 'almost' was to come back to haunt her with all that it left unsaid.

'I think the snow's finally stopped.'

It was early evening, and Jessica was drawing the curtains closed against the darkening night. If challenged, she would have been unable to say exactly how she had spent the hours since Daniel had spoken to his father. They had talked incessantly; she vaguely remembered eating, though what the meal had consisted of she couldn't recall; and of course they had made love again, that one, glorious coming together not enough to assuage their need of each other. Instead, it seemed as if it had opened the floodgates of the desire that had been smouldering between them unacknowledged ever since their very first meeting.

Daniel came to stand beside her, one arm, warm, heavy, and infinitely welcome, lying across her shoulders, cradling her against him, as he considered the snow-covered road with frowning concentration.

'It looks much more manageable now,' he agreed and, alerted by the reluctant note in his voice, Jessica turned questioning grey eyes on his face.

'Manageable?' she asked, feeling already the sense of loss in her heart because she knew what was coming.

'I have to go.' Daniel's quiet voice confirmed her fears.

To hide the sharp, stabbing pain that flashed through her, Jessica affected a small mock-pout, leaning her head against his chest and sliding one hand in at the open neck of his shirt, caressing the warm strength of muscle at his shoulder.

'Tomorrow,' she whispered, making her voice as sensually enticing as possible. Beneath her cheek she felt his chest shake with soft laughter.

'Tomorrow won't do—*Jess*!'

His voice rose in protest as her fingers wandered further, tracing delicate, erotic patterns on his skin. Daniel caught her roving hand in a firm grip and turned to look deep into her rebellious grey eyes, his expression gently serious.

'I *have* to go.'

'Sheffield's only a couple of hours' drive. Tomorrow——'

Daniel closed his eyes against her pleading look.

'You don't make it easy for me!' he groaned.

'I don't want to make it easy!' Jessica retorted mutinously. 'I don't want you to go.'

That earned her a kiss so soft and loving that she believed she had persuaded him to change his mind, but when Daniel lifted his mouth from hers he put her gently but firmly away from him.

'I *must* go, Jess. It isn't just a question of driving to Sheffield—though heaven knows how long that'll take in these conditions. I have to go to Doncaster first to collect my things. I didn't even check out of my hotel this morning, I was so determined to get here.'

Seeing her disappointed expression, he sighed and pushed a disturbed hand through his hair.

'Jess, please try and understand. This is how my life is right now. I'm a travelling man—here today, gone tomorrow. I have a career to think of. It's taken three long years to get this far; I can't afford to be considered unreliable, the sort of person who doesn't show up on time. Perhaps if——'

He caught himself up on what he had been about to say, but Jessica barely noticed. With a dull ache in her heart, all she could here were those ominous words: 'Here today, gone tomorrow.' While she had been dreaming of a new beginning, a future, Daniel had simply seen their lovemaking as a pleasurable but brief interlude in his life, to be forgotten once he moved on again.

'Ships that pass in the night.'

It was just a broken whisper, a tiny thread of sound, but Daniel caught it and his expression softened, his eyes deep and dark as they fixed on her face.

'Is that what you thought I meant? Oh, Jess, no! It isn't like that. I have to go now, but I'll come back whenever I can. I'm making no promises—it won't be easy, I'll be working almost every night——'

His hand came out and cupped her cheek, those dark eyes searching her face as if he wanted to reach into her mind and discover her innermost thoughts.

'It isn't perfect, but it's all I can offer at the moment. If you can't take it, then say so now.'

It wasn't enough! Jessica's heart cried. She wanted much more than the odd day he could spare from his career. She wanted *all* of him, wanted him with her every day. But if he wasn't the travelling man he had described, he wouldn't be Daniel—and it was Daniel she wanted.

'You'll come back?'

'When I can.' The beautiful voice was deep and sombre. 'I can't promise any more.'

It wasn't how she lived her life. She had always liked things organised, disciplined, so that she knew exactly where she stood. Could she be satisfied with seeing him only when his work left him free to come to her—snatching hours here and there, constantly saying goodbye, and never knowing when he would be back? Other women, whose husbands were at sea or in the Forces, coped with that way of life, but could she? For a brief, anguished moment she wanted to curse his career, wanted to cry out that if he cared he would abandon the stage and go back to being a lawyer, so that they could be together more often.

But immediately she caught herself up. Wasn't the fact that Daniel was prepared to go all out for what he wanted one of the things that had first attracted her to him? Jessica recalled how they had shared their feelings on the need for a challenge in life; how he had understood empathically her own thoughts on that subject. She couldn't take that challenge, that achievement, away from him. Being on the road was an essential part of Daniel. If she wanted him, she had to accept that.

'Jess?' Daniel prompted sharply, the urgency in his voice making her lift her head and look straight into his watchful, waiting eyes.

At once all her doubts and uncertainties evaporated like mist before the sun. Daniel was the man she wanted. A few hours spent with him was worth more than a lifetime with second-best.

'I can take it,' she said firmly. 'For you, I can take anything.'

CHAPTER NINE

THE JESTER was packed, every seat at every table taken, and Jessica looked round with a smile of satisfaction. Miriam had been right, the cabaret was a brilliant idea, and tonight—the smile widened—tonight had a very special significance because not only did it mark the beginning of the series of such acts which she planned to put on in the restaurant, but it was also the night on which Daniel was due to appear—the first of seven such nights, which meant that he would be in Scarby for the whole week. After months of brief, unsatisfactory meetings snatched out of Daniel's crowded days, that seemed like her own idea of heaven.

It had been harder to cope with Daniel's absences than she had ever anticipated. Life was just as full, and she was extremely busy. The restaurant was going from strength to strength, and she had even thought of expanding when the shop next door, whose lease was due to expire, came on to the market. She still had all her friends, she saw her family every week, but there was a strange sort of emptiness about her days, one that was at its worst on the days after Daniel's infrequent, fleeting visits.

That feeling had led her to make a completely uncharacteristic outburst at their last meeting, when Daniel had managed only two hours in her company. Following him out to his car to see him off, she had been overwhelmed by a sense of such total desolation that she had burst out impetuously, 'I don't want it to be like this!

There has to be a better way!' Turning to Daniel, she had caught his hands in hers and held them tightly. 'Why don't I come with you?'

But Daniel had shaken his head, his eyes darkly serious.

'It wouldn't work, Jess. It's a tough life, sometimes spending only one night here, another there. And besides, what would you do? You're a woman who needs a career—and I know how much you love your job.'

'I can cook anywhere!'

'But you couldn't have the Jester, and the Jester's your dream—the fulfillment of your ambition, just as comedy's mine. You couldn't abandon that, could you? You shouldn't have to, not for anyone.'

And there was no argument she could offer against that. The Jester was in her blood; it was part of her, something she had built up from scratch and watched grow into the thriving business it now was. And Daniel, damn him, knew that. He understood her better than she did herself. There was no way either of them could change without giving up a part of themselves; and so, much as she hated it, she resigned herself to things staying as they were.

But tonight Daniel was with her; tonight, and for six wonderful days after that. Jessica smoothed down the skirt of her cream silk dress and turned her mind to her duties as hostess, moving among the tables, smiling greetings, occasionally stopping to chat for a few moments. She lingered particularly at two special tables, one where her parents and brothers were gathered, and another, smaller one occupied by Melvyn and Kaye Tyson.

'Are you looking forward to tonight?' she asked, though there was no need for the question, for Daniel's father's feelings showed so clearly in his face. He still looked tired, his health was still causing some concern, but his eyes had lost that heavy, shadowed look, and that famous smile was always ready to surface on the slightest pretext. The longed-for reconciliation with his son had given him a new zest for life.

'Wouldn't miss it for the world!' he declared now, clearly revelling in his new role as Daniel Tyson's father—one Jessica strongly suspected he actually preferred to his own earlier fame. 'You've got a good turn-out, too.'

'Tonight and every other night.' Jessica nodded. 'We're booked solid between now and the end of the week. Daniel's really made a hit in Scarby.'

'And quite a few other places—I read the reviews. That young man is definitely going places!' Melvyn's pride in his son shone out of his eyes. 'I'm glad he was able to come here like this. It must have been hard for him to fit it in, seeing as he's so busy.'

That was one of the things that aggravated her own problems, Jessica reflected. As Daniel's popularity had increased, so had the demands on his time. The original free weeks in April had become non-existent, and it was only now, in early June, that he had managed to fulfil his promise to appear at the Jester.

'But he was determined to do this for you—it's a small way of thanking you for what you did for us both.'

'I was glad to help—and I think this week will benefit both Daniel and the restaurant.'

'I'm sure it will, and I'm glad.' It was Kaye who spoke. 'I know how much the Jester means to you.'

Her words made Jessica think of the poster Miriam had designed to advertise the cabaret. Unable to resist the link between Daniel's occupation and the name of

the restaurant, she had emblazoned them with the bold,
black headline, 'Jester at the Jester', bringing a small,
secret smile to Jessica's lips when she had seen them.

There were two jesters in her life now, the restaurant
and the man who would shortly appear on the small stage
erected in the centre of the dining-room—but only she
and Daniel knew that as yet. Their time together was so
short, so precious, that they hadn't told anyone about
their relationship, selfishly unwilling to share it with
anyone, which they would inevitably have to do when
the news finally leaked out—as it would very likely do
this week. They could hardly keep it a secret when Daniel
was in Scarby for seven days and, as he was staying with
his father and Kaye, his absences would very soon be
noticed.

'You can't believe how much it means to me to have
Daniel back in my home,' Melvyn Tyson was saying,
and, privately, Jessica thought she could guess. She had
only to look at Daniel, see the light in his eyes, the spring
in his step, to know that being reunited with his father
meant all the world to him.

Daniel and his father had had a long, private talk
about the past. He had told her some of what had passed
between them, and Jessica knew that Melvyn had admitted his faults and mistakes, apologising sincerely for
them. He had also acknowledged that, deep down, he
had known that Charlie was no good, and that, when
the shock and pain at seeing her and Daniel together had
worn off, he had come to suspect her part in things,
especially when he later discovered that she was having
an affair with a man two years younger than her. But
by then, of course, it was too late: he had lost all contact
with his son.

The new-found happiness the two men now shared had reconciled Jessica to her own personal disappointment when Daniel had told her that during his stay in Scarby he would be staying in his father's house. Dreamily anticipating long, love-filled nights and the luxury of a week of mornings waking up in his arms, something she had only managed on three memorable occasions so far, she had hoped that he would spend the week in her flat so that there would be no more partings, no wrenching goodbyes, for that brief time at least. But she understood how much his father's invitation meant to him, how staying under Melvyn's roof once more was the last stage in the healing of the terrible breach that had come between them for nine long years, and so she had swallowed down her protests, and was glad she had done so when she saw the happiness on Melvyn's face.

'I have to go,' she said, as Miriam's frantic signals from the opposite side of the room caught her eye. 'The show's about to start. Enjoy yourselves—and I'll see you later.'

A small room at the back of the restaurant had been converted into a tiny dressing-room for Daniel, and it was to this that she now made her way, knocking lightly on the door before pushing it open.

'It's nearly time to go on—are you ready?' she said as she made her way into the room. 'Daniel?' It came out on a note of concern and uncertainty when he didn't answer.

He was sitting in the room's only chair, his elbows resting on the shelf that served as a dressing-table, hands clasped together and his chin resting on them as he stared into the mirror straight in front of him, clearly seeing nothing of his own reflection, his eyes dark and broodingly abstracted.

'Daniel? Is something wrong?' she questioned sharply, and saw him start as if he had only just registered that she was in the room. Immediately a smile transformed the absorbed stillness of his face and, swinging round, he got to his feet.

After knowing him for some months, Jessica might have felt that the effect of his looks would have dimmed, the devastating physical impact softening with familiarity to something more gentle and easier to handle. Instead, it seemed as if every time she saw him his attraction struck her anew, and tonight just to look at him made her breath catch in her throat, her heart start to race in reaction.

She had never seen Daniel in formal evening clothes before, the superbly tailored black jacket and trousers seeming moulded on to his powerful frame, emphasising the glowing colour of his hair in contrast with their sombre tones, the immaculate white shirt throwing his harsh features into sharper relief while its fine material clung to the muscular contours of his shoulders and chest. Accustomed to his usual, comfortably casual clothes, Jessica found the effect of the formal elegance hit her like a blow to her stomach. She felt she had never seen a more beautiful, more complete man than the one who stood before her.

'No, nothing's wrong.' Daniel's voice jolted her out of her trance. 'I was just thinking—Jess——' He broke off abruptly, glanced at his watch and shook his head. 'No, not now,' he said, almost to himself.

'Not now what?'

Jessica was disturbed by the unexpected tension she could sense emanating from him. A shadowed look about his eyes and the way his hands moved restlessly, buttoning and unbuttoning his jacket, adjusting his bow-

tie, all betrayed an unease he was trying unsuccessfully
to hide. This wasn't the Daniel she knew, the relaxed,
confident man, self-assured and at ease with the world.

'I have something to tell you—but there isn't time
now.' He checked his watch again, quite unnecessarily,
because only seconds had passed since he had last looked
at it.

'Daniel, will you please tell me what's wrong?' Jessica
was really concerned now.

'Wrong?' Worryingly, his tone was suddenly taut and
sharp, then abruptly he laughed and a wry, self-
deprecatory smile crossed his face. 'Would you believe
I'm scared? Crazy, isn't it? I'm fine when I get on stage,
but beforehand I'm a nervous wreck. Look——'

He held out his hand and Jessica noted with some
shock the fact that it was visibly shaking. A powerful
sense of relief flashed through her.

'Is that all?' She caught his extended hand in both of
hers and squeezed it warmly. 'Dan, you'll be fine! You
know you will. You'll knock 'em dead.'

That lop-sided, self-derisory grin became more pronounced, bringing a boyishly vulnerable look to his face.

'Right now, what worries me is that *I'll* be the one
who dies when I get out there.'

'Not a chance!' Jessica declared confidently. 'You'll
be superb, as always.'

Was he always like this before a show? She had thought
she knew him, but there were still so many things she
had to discover about the complex strands that made up
the personality of Daniel Tyson. A warm glow lit her
heart at the thought that he had been so open, so honest
with her, even to the point of admitting something that
might have been interpreted as a weakness. She wanted
to take him in her arms, hold him tight, but, sensing

intuitively that that was not the right approach, aimed for a gently teasing support instead.

'Besides, I'll be rooting for you every step of the way.'

That earned her a genuine, unconstrained smile that went straight to her head like some potent spirit, leaving her floating in a state of glorious intoxication.

'Then how can I lose?'

And of course he had had no need to worry, Jessica thought a short time later when, having announced Daniel's act, she retreated to a quiet corner to watch the show. From the moment he strode out on to the stage, no trace of the crisis of nerves that had assailed him showing in his wide, confident smile, his self-assured bearing, he had the audience in the palm of his hand, just as she had known he would.

After having seen the way he had held a large audience entranced at the Civic Theatre, she was intrigued and delighted by the very different way Daniel handled the cabaret atmosphere. His tone was quieter, more intimate, at times almost conspiratorial as he let his glorious voice weave its spell over the diners. His stories were more satirical, often with a wry, pithy point to them, and there was none of the aching, exhausting laughter, just frequent chuckles of appreciation and a final, thunderous round of applause in appreciation of a point superbly well-made. She knew that everyone felt as she did—that they had been intellectually provoked as well as thoroughly, satisfyingly entertained.

At one point, half-way through the show, Jessica glanced up to find Tracey standing behind her, her eyes alight with laughter, a wide smile of appreciation on her face.

'Isn't he great?' the younger girl exclaimed. 'Don't you just *love* his show?'

No! Her instinctive response rocked Jessica's sense of reality, and she barely caught back the word in time to manage a smiling nod of agreement, her thoughts on another matter entirely.

No, she didn't love Daniel's act, she loved *Daniel*— all of him—not just the man on stage, the brilliant, skilful performer, but the lost and lonely man who had come to her on that snowy day, needing her help and not afraid or too proud to ask for it, the quiet, serious man who was such a contrast to the consummate artist now before her. She loved the man who had admitted to feeling afraid before his performance, the lover, passionate and yet gentle, who had brought her more pleasure than she had ever believed was possible. She *loved Daniel*.

Her grey eyes wide with wonder, Jessica turned back to the stage. What Daniel said, what stories he told, what laughter he provoked—none of it registered. All she knew was that this was the man she loved; all she saw was the wonderful human being who had made her life complete simply because he was part of it.

When the show had finished and Daniel had disappeared to his dressing-room, it was some time before Jessica could do what she most wanted, which was to join him there and congratulate him on his success in private—and then tell him how she felt. Everyone seemed to want to talk to her, to express their delight in the way the evening had gone, to recall particular highlights that had especially appealed to them, or simply to say how much they had enjoyed themselves. It seemed like hours before she finally managed to slip away and make her way down the dark, narrow passage to the rear of the restaurant.

The door to Daniel's dressing-room stood slightly ajar and Jessica caught the murmur of voices as she came closer—Daniel's familiar tones and another, a woman's voice—*Miriam's* voice!

Uncertainly Jessica hesitated. Through the half-open door she could see Daniel and her friend, their backs towards her—and Daniel's arm was around Miriam's shoulders, his other hand in hers.

'I can't tell Al yet, Dan. I'm not ready.' Miriam's voice was hesitant.

'He has to know some time.' The gentleness of Daniel's tone was like a blow to Jessica's heart. 'You *must* tell him.'

'I know that—but not yet! I'm scared——'

'But you can't leave it any longer, love. He'll have to know—and the sooner the better. He'll begin to suspect soon, if he doesn't already.'

Suspect. The word sounded alien, frightening on Daniel's lips. *Suspect?* What? Then, in a moment of realisation so sharp that it seared through her, Jessica knew just what it was that Al might begin to suspect— what *she* should have considered if she hadn't been so so foolishly, naïvely blind.

Daniel had explained about his stepmother, about the events of the past, and, deluded by her feelings for him, she had believed that he had explained everything. In her happiness over the past few months she had forgotten about Miriam—as she now saw she had been meant to forget.

Daniel knew she suspected him of trying to start an affair with Miriam, and so, with cold calculation, he had turned his attention to her in order to pull the wool over her eyes and distract her from what was really happening.

Jessica's mind went back to the few minutes she had spent with Daniel before his performance, recalling his obvious uneasiness. He had claimed to be nervous. Nervous! *Daniel!* She should have known. He had said he had something to tell her, just as Miriam now had something she had to tell Al. The room swung round her sickeningly. She had been *used*! Daniel hadn't cared for her at all. She had just been a smoke-screen, a cover to hide his real affair with Miriam. No wonder he hadn't wanted anyone to know they were together!

And now it seemed that they were ready to let their affair become public. Daniel had begun to tell her before he went on the stage but had reconsidered, knowing his timing was off. When could there ever be a right time for something like this? And now he was urging Miriam to tell Al.

At last, far too late, Jessica recalled how, on that Sunday afternoon when he had first made love to her, Daniel had said, 'I have almost everything I want.' That 'almost' now had a bite like acid, eating away at her heart. He had used her to make his peace with his father, he had her silence, having lulled her suspicions with his callous seduction, his false-hearted lovemaking—but he hadn't had everything he wanted because Miriam hadn't yet told Al that she was leaving him. *That* was what Daniel really wanted.

She didn't know how she made it to her office. She was shaking so much from shock and reaction that she couldn't believe that her legs had actually supported her on the short journey down the corridor. From the restaurant she could hear the sound of voices, the clink of plates and glasses, and knew that she should be out there, making sure that everything was going well, playing her role as hostess, but any such action was beyond her. She couldn't face anyone. All she wanted was to crawl into some deep, dark hole and lick her wounds in private.

But privacy wasn't granted to her for long. She didn't hear the quick, firm knock at her door; the tearing pain in her heart made her deaf and blind to her surroundings, so that the shock of Daniel's entrance was like a nuclear explosion in her mind.

He had changed out of the formal stage clothes and into the familiar casual shirt and jeans, and she couldn't stop her eyes from going to the lean, firm lines of his body, the harshly carved features, the wide, firm mouth that only a short time before had kissed her—so lovingly, she had believed.

'So this is where you've been hiding yourself. I've been looking for you everywhere.'

This was the Daniel she knew, every trace of the uncertainty she had seen earlier wiped from his face. But of course that nervousness had been a fraud, a mask as false as the warmth and affection she had believed—had deluded herself—he had shown to her. Anguish ripped through her so that she had to bite down hard on her lower lip to hold back the cry of pain that almost escaped her.

'What are you doing in here? Everyone's getting ready to leave—they're asking for you.'

The act was quite perfect. If she hadn't known the truth, Jessica would have sworn that he was the same man—the man she loved—and not the callous, uncaring monster who had taken her heart and shattered it into tiny pieces.

With a painful struggle Jessica drew on the tattered remnants of her emotional strength. Her pride, her hopes, her love, her life, all lay in ashes round her feet, but she wasn't going to let Daniel see that. He had come to tell her that it was over—that he and Miriam—— Her mind refused to finish the thought. There was only one way she could salvage something from this nightmare that had reached out to enclose her, and that was if *she* was the one to end the relationship.

Relationship! The word was like a scream of pain in her mind. There had been no relationship; it had been a lie from start to finish.

'Jess?' Daniel said quietly, questioningly, the softness of his voice acting like a goad to drive her into speech.

'I—needed time to think.'

'To think about what?'

'About—us.'

The tiny quaver in her voice that she hadn't been able to control had given her away, and she saw Daniel's quick frown.

'What about us?'

He looked genuinely taken aback; he must be a far better actor than she had ever given him credit for—or perhaps he suspected that she knew something of the truth and didn't know how she had come by that knowledge.

'It isn't working, Daniel!' The need to have the words spoken, to get it over with, made Jessica's voice high and sharp. 'I can't go on like this—it isn't the way I live my life.'

'I know it's been hard——'

It *had* been hard, at times she felt that it had been like a hell on earth, but, given the chance, she would have willingly endured those brief, unsatisfactory meetings, those constant separations, if it meant keeping him with her—if he'd always been the man she had fallen in love with. But she wasn't going to get that chance, and the thought that perhaps those meetings had been so brief, those separations so frequent because Daniel had been trying to divide what free time he had between herself and Miriam made her feel as if her heart was being slowly torn in two.

'But things can change. I——'

'*No!*'

Why was he doing this to her? Why didn't he just come right out and tell her? Did he think that if he manoeuvred her into ending the relationship then she would never tell anyone how badly he had treated her because she had been the one to break it off? Was that what he wanted? Did he think she was foolish enough to believe that his affair with Miriam had only started after she had said that *their* affair was over?

'I don't want it to change—I want it to end!' The last word almost choked her, but she forced it out. 'We're total opposites, Daniel, there's no point of contact in our lives. It isn't going to work and I don't *want* it to work! I want you to go and never see me again.'

'Jess!'

Jessica could have sworn that there was genuine pain in the way Daniel spoke her name. The thought that he was still acting out the lie twisted like a white-hot knife, so that in her agony she rounded on him savagely, feeling the years slip away as she flung at him almost the identical words to the ones she had used when she was eighteen.

'And I told you not to call me Jess! From now on it's Miss Terry to you!'

Even then he didn't take the chance to tell her the truth, but stuck to his act of hurt innocence.

'And to think I believed you were different,' he snarled. 'You couldn't change, Mystery—not in a lifetime!'

And when he had gone, the door slamming shut behind him, Jessica didn't know which hurt most—to know that she had lost him, or the fact that, right to the very end, he had never stopped lying to her.

Much as she wanted to stay hidden forever, Jessica forced herself to go out into the restaurant, pausing first to apply a little extra blusher to her unnaturally pale cheeks. Time enough to face the pain later; for now she must try to push it aside until the evening was over.

So she schooled her face into a mask of calm, even managed to smile and chat lightly with her family and friends, though inside she felt as if she were crumbling away, disintegrating into a heap of dust. She prided herself on the fact that no one noticed anything different about her, and saw the last person out of the door with a deep sigh of relief. The minute she was alone a wave of total exhaustion rocked her on her feet. Her shoulders sagged, her mind was a complete blank, she couldn't even begin to think how she was going to get home—and then, when she could least cope with it, she turned and saw Miriam and Al.

'Jess—we've something to tell you,' Miriam said softly, and Jessica longed to wrap her arms around herself to try to hold herself together, because she felt as if she were breaking into tiny pieces.

Not now! She couldn't take any more tonight. It was a struggle to make herself focus on the two of them, and what she saw shattered her sense of reality.

Al and Miriam were standing very close together, hand in hand, and the greatest shock was that Al's face was wreathed in smiles.

'Congratulate me, Jess!' he declared cheerfully. 'I'm going to be a dad.'

A dad! Jessica's eyes flew to Miriam's face, seeing the glow that lit it from inside, the warm, happy smile that curved her lips, and suddenly it was very hard to breathe.

'But I——'

'I thought it would never happen.' Al was oblivious to the way she had started to speak and then stopped abruptly. 'We've been trying for so long, I really believed there was something wrong. But at last it's all come right.'

'Jess?' Miriam's eyes were on her face. 'What is it?'

'I thought—you and Daniel——'

'Daniel?' Blank confusion showed on her friend's face, then, slowly, her expression changed. 'You thought there was something between us? Well, there was, but not in the way you think.' Impulsively she reached forward to take Jessica's hand. 'That night when you and I went to the theatre, I felt really down. We've been trying for a baby for ages, and the fact that I couldn't conceive has been a problem for some time—but after Christmas things got so much worse. Al——' she cast a loving look at her husband '—thought it was all his fault—he felt——'

'Inadequate,' Al supplied when she hesitated. 'And I took it out on you, working every hour God sent because I couldn't face going home.'

'Well, I can't have helped too much,' Miriam admitted honestly. 'I'd been taking my temperature to check if I was ovulating, and if it went up it had to be *now*, whether Al was in the mood or not.' Rosy colour flooded her cheeks.

'But, Miriam, why didn't you tell me?'

Jessica recalled Miriam saying that she and Al were thinking of trying for a baby, but there had been no mention of these other problems.

'Well, at first it didn't matter—I expected we'd have to wait a while before I got pregnant. But when it didn't happen I started to get uptight about the whole thing. I couldn't talk to anyone—not even Al—I wanted a child so much. And there were Al's feelings to consider.'

Jessica nodded slowly. She could understand that. Loving her husband as Miriam did, she would have been very reluctant to tell anyone anything that might have made him appear less than perfect.

'By the night we went to the theatre everything was getting on top of me—I had to talk to someone and I planned on telling you how things were over a drink, but Dan got in first. We had quite a while together while you were at the bar, and although I thought I was chatting away quite confidently, obviously the way I was feeling showed through. He guessed something was wrong and tried to get me to talk about it. He was so concerned—so gentle—and I thought that perhaps, as a man, he'd understand what Al was going through and be able to help me know how best to handle things.'

Miriam's earnest face blurred before Jessica's eyes. In her mind she was once more back in the theatre bar, seeing Miriam and Daniel so close together, watching him lean forward to take Miriam's hand in his.

'I was just about to let it all out when you joined us and the moment was lost, but when Dan took me home that night we talked for hours—and again when we went out to lunch the next day.'

'Then he came round one weekend and talked to me— helped me sort things out,' Al put in. 'Jess—are you all right?'

'I'm—fine,' Jessica managed shakily, though in fact her mind was in turmoil. She was reviewing all the events of those past days, seeing the relationship between Daniel and Miriam in a whole new light, and facing the fact of how blindly stupid she had been.

'A week ago I suspected I was pregnant,' Miriam went on. 'But I wasn't sure. I didn't dare tell Al in case I was wrong. I'd have kept it to myself even now, but tonight Daniel gave me a real talking to. He said Al had to know—that it wasn't fair to keep it from him.'

'And I thought——'

'You thought what? Oh, Jess—you didn't think we were having an affair, did you?'

Jessica flinched as Miriam put her finger unerringly on the truth, and knew from her friend's eyes that Miriam had seen the answer in her face.

'Don't you know it's *you* he's crazy about? He talks about you all the time. If ever a man was head over heels in love, it's Daniel Tyson—and you're the one he's fallen for.'

'*In love?*' Jessica's voice was just a whisper, but the next minute it rose to a pained cry. 'But, Miriam, I sent him away!'

'You did what? Oh, Jess, no! When did this happen? Tonight?'

Miriam's grip on Jessica's hands tightened sharply.

'Why did you do such a thing?'

'I was blind—I thought——' The words wouldn't come, but she knew they weren't needed. Miriam could fill in all she couldn't say.

'But now you know the truth, you can't let him think you don't love him—because you do, don't you?—it's written all over your face. Jess, you must go to him, tell him——'

Go to him. Her own words spoken to Daniel when he had asked what to do about his father, and, as she had then, Jessica knew they were the right ones. But would Daniel listen? Her rejection must have hurt him terribly. And where would she find him? At his father's? No. Things were still too new and fragile between them; intuitively she knew that Daniel wasn't yet ready to share his deepest, most personal feelings with Melvyn. So *where*?

Suddenly she knew. The thought of Melvyn Tyson had reminded her of the day she had spent on the moors with Daniel, and the spot overlooking his father's home where Daniel had said he used to go. 'This was my hiding-place whenever things got on top of me.'

Suddenly Jessica pulled her hands from Miriam's grasp.

'I have to go,' she said, and saw the deepest understanding on her friend's face.

'Of course you do. Find Daniel, Jess. Find him and tell him you love him.'

He *had* to be there! Oh please, *please*, God, let him be there, Jessica prayed as she turned her car on to the road that led to the moors, driving at a reckless speed in the darkness. She took the direct route this time, taking the lane that led to the bottom of the cliff, a huge sigh of relief escaping her as her headlights picked out a dark shape at the side of the road—Daniel's car.

It was pitch-black, but there was a torch in the glove compartment. It didn't give much light, but it would have to do. Her feet slipped and stumbled on the rough tussocks of grass, and once she fell back several feet, letting out a yelp of fright as she tumbled downwards.

Was he there? He had to have heard her, or seen her car's lights, so why didn't he *say* something? He must know that no one else was aware of this special place.

'Hello, Mystery.'

The quiet voice came so suddenly out of the darkness that her heart leapt in fright. Hearing the sardonic greeting, the old cynical nickname, she knew just what she had done to him, how much she had hurt him, and a terrible sense of guilt made her voice shake as she answered him.

'Where are you? I can't see a thing——'

But then the weak beam of her torch picked out the dark, shadowy figure above her, feet planted firmly apart, his arms folded across his broad chest, his whole stance, every inch of his tautly held body declaring his hostility more clearly than any words. Jessica couldn't see his face, it was hidden in the darkness, and she didn't dare let her torch travel up that far for fear of what she might read in his eyes.

'What do you want?' The hard-toned voice was definitely discouraging.

'To talk——'

Jessica broke off sharply as she slipped again and had to grab at a clump of heather to stop herself from falling all the way to the bottom. Her elegant leather sandals with their two-inch heels were not designed for hill-climbing—in fact, they were positively lethal.

'Here——' Daniel said gruffly, holding out his hand to her.

Jessica grasped it thankfully, letting him haul her bodily up the last few feet until, breathless and dishevelled, she reached the top.

As soon as she was safely at his side, Daniel let her hand drop abruptly, the gesture stabbing straight to

Jessica's heart with its eloquent testimony to the way he was feeling.

'Daniel...'

She didn't know where to begin, what to say. She still found it impossible to breathe naturally, all the air seeming to be trapped low down in her lungs, but it was no longer the effort of the climb that caused the reaction, rather the overwhelming sense of Daniel's closeness. He was only inches away from her, but the tension in every muscle, the silent withdrawal, made her feel that they might be at opposite ends of the earth.

With a sudden, startling move, Daniel took the torch from her limp grasp and let it travel slowly up from her battered and soiled shoes and over her grass-stained dress, halting at her throat.

'Your dress is ruined.'

There was an odd note in his voice, a husky rawness, as if he spoke from a painfully sore throat, that gave a whole new dimension to the trivial words.

'I don't give a damn about my dress!' Jessica declared, then blinked violently as the full force of the light was directed stright into her face, blinding her momentarily.

'Why have you come here, Jessica?' Daniel demanded harshly.

And suddenly it was so very easy, as she had told Daniel about his father, and as Miriam had told her—all she had to do was say it.

'To tell you that I love you,' she stated, clearly and firmly.

The beam of the torch wavered as his hand clenched on it. She couldn't see his face, but the silence beyond the light told her that her words had hit home.

'I love you, Daniel—*love* you! I know I told you to go—get out of my life—but I didn't mean it. I was slightly out of my mind because I thought—I saw you with Miriam and I thought——'

'Miriam!'

The hand that held the torch jerked convulsively as he repeated the name on a note of shocked disbelief.

'*Miriam!* Did I go to Miriam when I needed help? Was it Miriam who healed the breach between my father and me? Did I make love to *Miriam*?'

'No—no! Oh, Daniel, I know now I was wrong.' At last the constraint on her tongue seemed to have eased and the words came tumbling out like a swiftly flowing river. 'I know I've been blind and indescribably foolish—but I wasn't thinking straight. I'm so desperately sorry for the way I treated you—I know the pain it must have brought you, but I never meant to do it. I didn't know—I never wanted to hurt you, Daniel. I love you!'

'And I love you, you crazy idiot!'

Unheeded, the torch fell to the ground as he reached out to pull her into his arms, but they needed no light, their lips meeting unerringly as Daniel held her close, subjecting her to a kiss so full of love and passion that the stars seemed to spin around her, dancing in the midnight sky above them.

'I love you,' Daniel whispered huskily against her hair when he finally released her. 'You're my world, my life—my love.'

The hug that enveloped her drove all the breath from her body, threatening to crush her bones with its intensity, but Jessica didn't care. She was lost in a world of delight, oblivious to anything else. The coldness of the night couldn't touch her; she was glowing from head to toe, warm and safe in Daniel's love. There was nothing more she could want.

'Jess.' Daniel's beautiful voice was low and intent. 'Jess, will you marry me, be with me forever?'

'I'll be with you forever, no matter what. I don't need marriage.'

'But I *do*.'

The sudden roughness of his voice told her how much this meant to him—and of course Daniel did need the commitment of marriage. After his parents' break-up, the distance that had come between him and his father, the long, lonely years that had followed, he needed that affirmation of how they felt for each other. She had opened her mouth to give him his answer when Daniel spoke again.

'Before you say anything, I have something to tell you. I was going to say this tonight anyway, but there wasn't time before the show, and afterwards——'

A violent shake of his head dismissed the distressing events of the evening as over and done with.

'I know how hard you've found these last few months—I've hated it too. I've wanted you with me all the time. If you knew how every night I've lain awake, imagining what it would be like to fall asleep in your arms, wake up to find you there——'

'Daniel——' Jessica lifted a hand to lay it across his lips to silence him. 'It doesn't matter.'

She spoke urgently, emphatically, filled with a sudden fear that he might be about to tell her that he was giving up his stage career and going back to being a lawyer. He couldn't do that—he mustn't! His comedy was pure genius! It was what he had been born to do—he couldn't give that up for her. 'You mustn't think of giving up being a comic, Daniel! I won't let you—it's in your

blood. You wouldn't be the man you are without it—
and that man is the one I love. I told you, I can cope
with anything if I have you. I want to be with you under
any circumstances. I want to be your wife.'

'Some marriage, if we're together once in a blue
moon!' Daniel exclaimed. 'But what I'm trying to tell
you is that it doesn't have to be like that any more. Do
you remember that when I had to change the dates of
the cabaret I said I had to go to Manchester? I had an
interview with some television people. I've been writing
some scripts . . .' His tone altered, becoming slightly wry.
'There isn't much else you can do to while away the time
in a hotel room.'

'They've accepted them?' Jessica interrupted, unable
to control her excitement. Her heart lifted as she saw his
nod.

'And more. In August I start work on a series—my
own show, Jess! It's happened at last—and it couldn't
have come at a better time. I'll be able to stay put at
last, look for a house up here—but, best of all, we'll be
together.'

Together. Jessica felt tears of happiness sting her eyes.
Together—it had such a wonderful sound.

'Oh, Daniel, I'm so happy for you—so happy and so
proud!'

'Not half as proud as I'll be on the day I can call you
my wife.'

With his arm around her waist, Daniel turned to look
in the direction of his father's house.

'And if you agree, then maybe one day we'll give my
father those grandchildren he's been talking about.'

'We will,' Jessica promised softly, her mind full of
wonderful images of the time when the breach between

Daniel and his father would finally be completely healed by the creation of a whole new family.

She heard Daniel draw in his breath as if he were about to speak, and intuitively sensed his need without a word having to be spoken.

'Let's go and tell him now.'

Even in the darkness, Daniel's wide, loving smile was clear to her eyes.

'We'll tell him,' he said softly. 'But first . . .'

His lips came down hard on hers, hungry and demanding, and she met that demand willingly, her whole body coming gloriously, vividly alive as he lifted her off her feet and crushed her against him.

'That, my darling restaurateur,' he whispered huskily, his breath warm on her cheek, 'was just a taste of the aperitif—the main course is yet to come.'

'I can't wait,' Jessica assured him breathlessly, feeling her need and desire uncoiling itself deep inside her. 'Because I suddenly find that I'm very, very hungry.'

'So am I.' Daniel's voice was a low, sensual growl. 'So let's get started straight away. First we tell my father, and then . . .'

He let the sentence trail off, but there was no need for him to finish it; the promise in his voice told her all she needed to know, and her heart soared in delight as, with her hand held firmly in his, they turned and went down the slope together.

From *New York Times* Bestselling author
Penny Jordan, a compelling novel of ruthless passion
that will mesmerize readers everywhere!

Penny Jordan

Silver

Real power, true power came from
Rothwell. And Charles vowed to have it,
the earldom and all that went with it.

Silver vowed to destroy Charles, just as surely and
uncaringly as he had destroyed her father; just as he had
intended to destroy her. She needed him to want her . . .
to desire her . . . until he'd do anything to have her.

But first she needed a tutor: a man who wanted no one.
He would help her bait the trap.

Played out on a glittering international stage,
Silver's story leads her from the luxurious comfort of
British aristocracy into the depths of adventure,
passion and danger.

AVAILABLE IN OCTOBER!

 HARLEQUIN
®

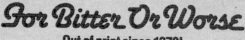

You'll flip . . . your pages won't!
Read paperbacks *hands-free* with

Book Mate • I

The perfect "mate" for all your romance paperbacks

Traveling • Vacationing • At Work • In Bed • Studying
• Cooking • Eating

Perfect size for all standard paperbacks, this wonderful invention makes reading a pure pleasure! Ingenious design holds paperback books OPEN and FLAT so even wind can't ruffle pages – leaves your hands free to do other things. Reinforced, wipe-clean vinyl-covered holder flexes to let you turn pages without undoing the strap . . . supports paperbacks so well, they have the strength of hardcovers!

Pages turn WITHOUT opening the strap.

SEE-THROUGH STRAP

Reinforced back stays flat

Built in bookmark!

BOOK MARK

BACK COVER HOLDING STRIP

10" x 7¼", opened.
Snaps closed for easy carrying, too.